MW01232007

McKenna's Honor

Book Four of The Clan MacDougall Series
A Novella

Suzan Tisdale

McKenna's Honor

Cover by Seductive Designs
Cover Images by: Jenn LeBlanc/Illustrated Romance
and Tomáš Šereda

Suzan Tisdale

DEDICATION

3

CONTENTS

ACKNOWLEDGMENTS

I know first that I would not be where I am today were it not for the love and support of my loving husband, children, and family. They are a blessing.

I want to also thank some of the most amazing women that I have ever had the pleasure of knowing: My street team, *Suzan's Highland Lassies*. Their excitement and enthusiasm is contagious and inspires me to get it done. Sadly, we lost one of our lassies this spring. Carol will be missed beyond measure. Her infectious laughter, her wit, and her love of reading are just a few of the things that made her so special.

I would also like to thank author Tarah Scott. She gives of herself and her time to newbies like me. I love her sense of business and her outlook on writing, and her wicked, wicked sense of humor! She also writes some pretty terrific books!

A very special thanks to Tanya Anne Crosby. If you like the book description/blurb for McKenna's Honor, you can thank Tanya. Graciously, she helped me write it. (I don't like writing the blurbs!) Tanya is one of the sweetest, funniest women that I know. And she writes amazing books too!

I want to also thank my beautiful readers and fans. Without all of you, I would not be living this dream of mine. Words cannot express my appreciation, admiration, and love for each and every one of you. Thank you.

PROLOGUE

An old adage declares there is no honor among thieves. The same can be said of traitors. Traitors often hide in the open, in plain sight. The truth is there for people who choose to see it, for those who are determined to see things as they are and not as they wish them to be.

In reality, traitors are nothing more than pretenders. Master manipulators. Actors in a play in which only they know who is who and what is what.

The people around them are but an audience, often seeing only what they *wish* to see.

When a traitor performs, openly defending the weak, speaking only with highest regard for his king and country and displaying an unequaled façade of honor, well, who would question his fealty? The traitor reveals only what he *wishes* others to see and only what he knows they wish to believe.

All the while the traitor silently laughs at the folly he has created, taking great pleasure in the absurdity of the entire situation.

And if he is extremely careful the world will never know who or what he *truly* is.

However, as is often the case with thieves, traitors, and ne'er-do-wells, fate steps in at the most unexpected times. It rips away the heavy curtain of subterfuge and duplicity, to openly display to the world not what it wishes to see, but what it in fact *must* see.

Such inaugurations to the truth are often painful and traumatic, leaving the newly inaugurated feeling stunned, stupefied and bitter. For some, the only means of survival is outright denial. They shun the truth, cursing it, preferring instead to live in denial. Mayhap because they love the traitor so much, it is easy to justify the traitor's behavior. Or, they may not wish to believe they could have been so easily duped.

But as in all good plays, there are subtle twists and turns. Some are quite obvious, others, not so much. Mayhap the truth isn't always what it seems. Mayhap there is far more to it than anyone realizes.

What then, motivates a man? A man like Angus McKenna who has spent his life defending the defenseless, offering hope to the hopeless, lifting up the weak? Honorable. Honest. Steadfast. A leader of men. A man loyal to king and country. A man above reproach. This is the man Angus McKenna's people see, the man other leaders see, the man the world sees.

Ever since the day he took his oath as chief of the Clan MacDougall and made the promise to uphold and protect his clan above all other things, Angus McKenna put his family and his clan first. Each decision he made since that fateful day in 1331 was made with only one thought in mind: how will it affect his family and his clan?

Nothing mattered but the safety and wellbeing of his people. Not his own comfort, his own desires nor his own needs could be taken into consideration when making decisions that would directly affect his people.

What could have made Angus McKenna don a red and black plaid and turn against his king? His country? How could a man like Angus McKenna do such a thing? What could be of such a value that he would plot to murder his king and to forge a pact with the English? A pact that would cause the fall of his country and put it squarely into the hands of the very people he has spent his entire life fighting against.

Gold? Silver? Power? Something more?

Time and experience reveal that things are not always as they appear.

ONE

Edinburgh, Scotland, Summer 1347

"Angus McKenna, ye stand before this tribunal today, accused of crimes against our king and the country of Scotland," the under-sheriff read from the document he held in his thin, trembling hands. He paused, looking toward the dais where the leader of the tribunal, the Sheriff of Edinburgh, sat.

The under-sheriff was a scrawny man, with bloodshot eyes and pale skin. With dark circles under his bloodshot eyes, he looked as though he had not slept in days. He stood in direct contrast to the sheriff, who was a rotund, portly man.

After a heavy sigh and a wave of a hand from the sheriff, the under-sheriff continued. His dull eyes darted about the room, looking everywhere but at Angus McKenna.

Coward, Angus thought to himself. *He does no' have the courage to look me in the eye.* Angus found the man's demeanor amusing.

"How do you plead to these charges?" the under-sheriff asked. Angus noted the slight tremble in the man's voice, as if he were not only afraid to ask the question, but also to hear Angus' answer.

Angus stood tall and proud, ignoring the fact that his hands and feet were shackled. He looked the sheriff straight in the eyes when he answered.

"Guilty."

His reply was loud and firm. He was determined to remain that way, no matter what the outcome might be. Admittedly, he *had* done all the things of which he was accused. There was no denying the accusations let alone the charges. He *had* conspired against his king, his country.

Angus did not care for the arrogant sheriff, what with his fancy ways, false airs and his unearned pride. Phillip Lindsay was a haughty fool, with a mean streak as long as a summer day in the Highlands. It was difficult for Angus to believe the man was the son of Carlich Lindsay, his longtime friend and ally.

The under-sheriff's eye began to twitch, as he looked first at Angus and then to Phillip. He seemed to shrink, to draw himself inward as if he were afraid the floor beneath his feet would open up and swallow him whole. The tall scrawny man waited for the sheriff to say something.

Phillip Lindsay sitting with his head resting against his pudgy index finger seemed unmoved by Angus' answer. If he took any joy in the matter, it did not show. Indifferent and mayhap a bit disgusted. Whether with Angus or the proceedings was difficult for him to ascertain. *No matter*, Angus thought to himself. It also did not matter how he pleaded to the charges. Phillip Lindsay would have found him guilty anyway regardless of any claim of innocence Angus might have made.

Before either the sheriff or under-sheriff could speak, Duncan McEwan, Angus' son-in-law spoke up. His shackles rattled as he took a step forward to stand next to Angus. Although the man was covered in dirt and grime, his blonde hair hanging in filthy strings about his face, his blue eyes still held the look of a proud Highland warrior. He stood straight and tall, proud, and dignified. The fool was as stubborn as Angus, something he had learned no doubt from watching Angus all these years.

"I plead guilty as well," Duncan said with more than just a hint of pride to his voice.

The under-sheriff was startled by Duncan's voice as it boomed through the room. His eyes blinked rapidly for a moment before he found the courage to speak. "Ye need to wait yer turn, Duncan McEwan."

Duncan tilted his blonde head to the side and smiled deviously at the skinny man in charge of keeping him and Angus in chains. "Why?" Duncan asked. "The charges be the same fer me as fer Angus. I simply be savin' ye time and breath."

"Silence," Phillip Lindsay ordered in a calm voice. "Ye'll get yer turn soon enough, ye traitor."

Before Duncan could respond to the insult, Angus pulled tight on the shackles to keep the young man in place and from making a deadly mistake. "Hold, son," he whispered firmly.

Duncan pursed his lips together and drew his shoulders back. His dark blue eyes flickered with silent understanding. He gave a nod of affirmation before turning back to the under-sheriff.

"Ye both are accused of crimes against the king, against the great country of Scotland. Ye planned and plotted with the English to murder our king. Ye've both admitted to such." Phillip Lindsay spoke from the dais, his voice carried through the half-empty room. One would have thought throngs of people would be in attendance this day, considering the charges and the circumstances. Mayhap it was the rain that kept the usual anxious, excited onlookers away. Angus did not think it was the rain that kept people away. Nay, it was something more, something he could not quite put his mind to. Those few men in attendance were drawn to Phillip Lindsay's deep voice and turned their attention to him.

Phillip continued to stare at Angus, looking ashamed to call Angus a Scot. *So be it,* Angus thought as he straightened his back and lifted his head high. He would not let a man like Phillip Lindsay make him feel regretful, ashamed or humiliated.

Phillip Lindsay's upper lip curled slightly, as if he were standing too near a pile of horse dung. After several long moments, he let out a sigh of disgust and sat himself upright in his ornately carved chair.

Angus did not believe for one moment that Phillip Lindsay was actually mulling over the charges. Nor did he fight with his conscience over the sentence he should mete out to Angus or Duncan. Nay, 'twas all nothing more than a show for the few men sitting on the benches as witnesses. 'Twas nothing more than play acting, and the sheriff was the bard, a teller of stories.

"I hereby sentence ye both to death. One week from today, ye shall be taken to Stirling, where ye will both be hanged by yer necks until dead," he declared to those observing the tribunal. "Get the traitors out of me sight," he ordered the under-sheriff.

Reluctantly, almost solemnly, the under-sheriff led Angus and Duncan out of the dark room. Three of his men were waiting outside. Once in the hallway, the trio surrounded Angus and Duncan and led them out of the building and into the courtyard.

It had been days since Angus and Duncan had seen the sun. From the looks of the gloomy sky and the steady rain that fell, it would be even longer before they would see it again.

Though a number of people huddled in the rain, none would look at Angus or Duncan. Angus wondered if it was fear that kept their eyes cast to the ground or mayhap and much worse, *shame.*

It was of his own doing. He *had* shamed his people, his family, and his reputation. There was no denying this. No one, save mayhap for the young man chained to him, would understand the reasons for what he had done. The choice had been his to make three years past and made it he had.

The only guilt Angus felt at the moment was the fact that Duncan was here with him. Duncan was his adopted son as well as his son-in-law. Duncan was just a boy when his family had been killed by a band of English soldiers who had attacked his village. Only three boys had survived the ordeal, two of which were Angus' nephews by blood. The boys had come to live with him and Isobel and not long after, they had adopted all three lads.

Angus and Isobel had adopted several children over the years, but together, they had only one flesh and blood daughter. Angus did, however, have another daughter whom he had long thought dead, along with her beautiful mum. Through circumstances not of his choosing, he did not learn of her existence until three years ago and then not until after Duncan and Aishlinn had fallen hopelessly in love with one another.

The young man did not deserve to be here for he was no more a traitor in this macabre mess Angus had gotten into than Mother Mary. 'Twas Duncan's own stubbornness that brought him here and nothing more.

Soon they came to the entrance to the dungeon. When the under-sheriff opened the heavy wooden door, the smell of filth, death and despair assaulted their senses. The skinny man grabbed a lit torch from the brace on the wall and led the way down the filthy, damp stone stairs. Through a maze of twists and turns, they made their way to the bowels of the dungeon. They passed numerous cells filled with all sorts of lost souls. Men, and aye, even a few women, who had lost all hope long ago.

Some were thieves, some murderers, and some whose only guilt was being poor and uneducated. Compassion for the poor and uneducated tugged at Angus' heart. It was through no fault of their own that they were here. If Angus had had any control over the current situation, he'd have done what he could to free them and send them to Gregor, to give them a chance at a somewhat decent life.

Nay, 'twas not to be. Not today. Nor at any time in the foreseeable future.

He could not help them any more than he could help himself at the moment and the thought pulled at his heart.

Once Angus and Duncan stepped into their cell, the door was closed behind them. Even though they were given a private cell and not tossed in with the murderers, both men knew they were not necessarily safe from harm.

While the under-sheriff appeared both afraid and sympathetic, Angus knew the other guards held no such feelings toward them. And with all that had taken place since the battle at Neville's Cross last October, it was sometimes difficult to tell who was friend and who was foe.

For three long years, Angus had been playing the role of spy and traitor. He had played it so well that the lines had begun to blur. It had been a very fine line he had walked, a very fine line indeed.

And after the events at Neville's Cross Angus knew that *no one* could be trusted.

TWO

Angus hangs at dawn.

No matter how many times Nial McKee read the missive he held in his hand, he could not grasp the reality of it. Surreal. Unbelievable.

Angus McKenna, one of the most honorable men he'd ever known, his own father-in-law for the sake of Christ. And he had not only been accused of treason and crimes against their king, he had admitted to them!

Why? Why would the most respected and revered chief of one of the mightiest clans in Scotland do such a thing?

Nial ran a hand through his short brown hair, tossed the missive onto his desk and finally looked up at Caelen McDunnah, the man who had brought him the news.

Caelen had been Nial's best friend for as long as he could remember. To anyone who did not know the two men well, their friendship was a curious one, for no two men could be more dissimilar.

Where Nial was short and stocky, with short-cropped light brown hair and gray blue eyes, Caelen was tall and built like a wall of stone. He wore his nearly black hair long, with braids on either side of his temples, and his dark brown eyes, rarely, if ever, sparkled. Where Nial's body was relatively free of scars, a rough, jagged scar ran from Caelen's forehead, down the left side of his face, and ended a few inches under his left armpit.

Nial knew it should have been *his* face and body marred by that scar, not Caelen's.

Their friendship had begun not long before the Battle of Berwick in 1333. They'd been very young men, anxious to prove to themselves and to the world their abilities on the battlefield. Both men had come close to dying at Berwick. Much blood -- a good portion of it belonging to Caelen -- along with their youthful exuberance and immature lust for fighting was left on that marshy battlefield.

Since that day, Nial had done everything he could to avoid fighting. Nay, he was no coward, for he would fight to his own death if the circumstances called for it. He had fought in too many battles to count. But whenever possible, he would give diplomacy a chance before drawing his sword.

The same could not be said for Caelen. The man enjoyed a good fight. It was often said that he would sometimes start an argument for the sole purpose of brawling. Whether it was boredom or some twisted, inner desire to test fate and death, one couldn't be certain. For whatever reason, Caelen enjoyed fighting.

"I couldna believe it meself when I first read it," Caelen said from the opposite side of Nial's desk. Nial found it difficult at the moment to ascertain what Caelen might truly be thinking. Nial was one of the very few people who could read Caelen's moods and sometimes thoughts, regardless of any outward expression. But today, Caelen's thoughts were indiscernible.

Nial's principal worry however, was his wife, Bree, and how she would take the news of her father's incarceration and the charges leveled against him. *This is going to kill Bree,* he thought to himself.

"Where is Duncan in all of this?" Nial asked, his voice sharp and full of concern.

Caelen cleared his throat and crossed well-muscled arms over his broad chest and leaned against the fireplace mantle. "Sittin' right next to his treasonous father-in-law."

Nial's eyes widened with surprise and shock. It was bad enough that his brother-in-law also sat in the dungeon in Edinburgh. Caelen knew the two men as well as Nial. He was astonished to hear Caelen refer to either man as a traitor. "Certainly ye dunna believe Angus a traitor?"

Caelen cocked his head as he chewed on the inside of his cheek. "He's admitted to it, Nial. Both have."

Nial's eyes turned to small slits. "I do no' believe it. I will no' believe it until I speak to them." *How in the name of God am I goin' to tell Bree?*

Angus and Duncan. Accused of treason. That either man would admit to such a thing would be laughable, were they not both sitting in a dungeon in Edinburgh, waiting to be hanged. Nial had known these men most of his life. Never, not once in all that time had either of them done anything, said anything, or otherwise acted in any manner that would make anyone question their loyalty to Scotland or her king.

"Where are Isobel and Aishlinn?" Nial asked as he tried to make sense of the news.

"That be a good question," Caelen began. "I was hopin' they were here."

More confusion knitted on Nial's brow. "Nay, we've not seen any of them in many months." Clarity began to dawn as he studied his friend more closely. There was something to Caelen's countenance and his voice that gave Nial pause. "Ye dunna ken where they are?" It was more a statement than a question.

"Nay, we do no' ken where they be. It seems they disappeared the same night that the sheriff's men came fer Angus and Duncan. The babes be missin' too." Caelen looked pained to tell Nial that last bit of news.

"Disappeared?" Unease and worry began to double. His stomach suddenly felt heavy, filled with the dread of having to explain all of this to his sweet wife. *Bree.*

Caelen remained silent for a time, allowing Nial time to come to terms with the news that two of his in-laws were admitted traitors and their female counterparts, along with his nephews were missing.

With a scrutinizing gaze, pursed lips, and furrowed brow, Nial tried to read Caelen's face. What exactly *wasn't* he telling him? He could not quite put his finger to it, but there *was* something hidden, something Caelen was deliberately keeping from him.

The men watched each other closely for several long moments. The only sound in the room came from the crackling fire and the soft rain as it fell against the shutters of the keep.

Nial hoped for some sign of what his friend might be thinking. It suddenly dawned on him that there was a strong possibility that Caelen worried that Nial too, might be less than loyal to their king. "Ye think me a traitor as well? Is that why ye be here Caelen?" He made no attempts to hide his anger or his disgust. "Ye ken I be no more a traitor than ye!"

"What of Angus' admission?" Caelen asked. His voice was calm. Holding not even the slightest hint as to what he was thinking or feeling.

Nial let out an exasperated sigh. "What of it?" he barked. "There must be a reason fer him to admit to such a thing." Nial would never believe Angus or Duncan was a traitor.

"Each has admitted to it, Nial. The question be *why*? Be it the truth, or something more?"

In his heart, Nial knew there could be no truth to the accusations. He turned to gaze out the window behind his desk. Dawn was just beginning to break beyond the horizon. Green as far as his eye could see save for the ewes and their lambs that dotted the summer grass. On this rainy day, the sheep looked like gray clouds that had fallen to the earth.

Below stairs, the keep was slowly coming to life. Soon the younger maids would begin to light the fires in the gathering room and the kitchen staff would begin preparing the morning meal. Within the hour, the many inhabitants of the keep would begin scurrying about with their daily duties.

The early morning hours had always been Nial's favorite time of day. He loved waking up and pulling Bree into his arms and holding her close to his chest. Sometimes, if he woke early enough, he would have time to show her just how much he adored and cherished her before their son woke and demanded her full and undivided attention.

He would not relish waking her this morn. Nay, he would let her sleep until Jamie woke. Nial imagined it would be some time before they slept in blissful, untroubled, contented sleep again.

Bree was just four doors away from where he now stood. Their seven-month-old son Jamie was fast asleep in his cradle just steps away from their bed. Nial wished he could climb back into bed with his wife and forget that Caelen had not just delivered him such dire news.

"I tell you, there has to be a reason, but I dunnae what it be." Nial said, still trying to come to terms with the news.

Caelen straightened himself and came to stand before Nial's desk.

"What can ye think of that would get men like Angus McKenna and Duncan McEwan to admit to treason? If it be not the truth, then what?"

Nial thought on the question for a time, his lips pursed together as a hard line formed above his brows. There could be only one reason, other than the truth, that would elicit Angus' confession.

"Isobel," Nial murmured. Isobel was Angus' wife, Bree's mum, and the love of Angus McKenna's life.

"Aishlinn, Bree," Caelen offered, "his grandchildren." He waited patiently for his friend Nial to join his own way of thinking.

Nial turned to face Caelen. Only a moment passed before realization began to sink in. Angus and Duncan were protecting their wives and families. Nothing else made sense. Nial noticed a twinkle of sorts present in Caelen's deep brown eyes. For those who did not know the man well, they might have thought it something malevolent, but Nial knew better. Relief enveloped Nial as he came to the sudden conclusion that Caelen did not think Angus McKenna a traitor any more than Nial did.

"Ye do no' think Angus a traitor," Nial said.

Caelen smiled and shook his head. "No more than I think ye be."

Suddenly, Nial felt hopeful and encouraged. Caelen's twinkling eyes said enough. There might just be hope for Angus and Duncan after all. Nail smiled, his spirits lifting considerably. But it was short lived.

Aye, Caelen may well have a plan, something as yet unspoken, that might, just *might* help the two men he admired most in life. But he still had to break the news to Bree. He knew it would be one of the most difficult conversations of his life.

Nial took a deep breath and steeled himself for his wife's reaction to the news that her father was an admitted traitor. Her reaction was not what he had expected. They had been married for a year and a half and he knew there was still much to he needed to learn about the woman who was his sole reason for living.

He had expected her to be outraged and appalled that anyone would accuse her father of such misdeeds. He fully expected her to stomp about their bedchamber, furious, and demanding action. And if Nial wouldn't put the call out to bring their warriors to arms, she would do it herself.

Instead, his strong, beautiful wife sat in a chair beside the fireplace watching their son Jamie as he suckled at her breast. She seemed unmoved by the news. Her calm demeanor, her quite façade scared the hell out of him. Aye, she may have responded in a quiet and dignified manner, but Nial felt certain she was quietly plotting the deaths of the person or persons who had accused her father and Duncan of such atrocities.

Bree smiled proudly at Jamie as she spoke to her husband. "And what do we intend to do about it?" she asked without looking up.

Nial stood speechless for a moment. He supposed she was keeping her anger in check for fear of upsetting their babe.

"Caelen waits fer me below stairs," he began. "We do no' know yet who is behind this. They canna find Isobel or Aishlinn and the babes."

Bree's head shot up at that piece of news. "What do ye mean they canna find them?"

"They went missin' the same night they came to take Angus and Duncan away," Nial told her as he bent to one knee beside her. He ran a hand over his son's dark locks. Under normal circumstances he would have felt a tad jealous that his son was enjoying that part of Bree that Nial found pleasure with as well.

Bree reached out and gently laid a hand on Nial's arm. She needed his reassurance that all would be well. Although she was worried for her father and Duncan, her stomach drew into knots with worry over where Isobel and Aishlinn were. Who knew where they might be and what they were going through. She did her best to chase those terrifying thoughts away. She knew she'd be no good to them, or anyone else, if she could not keep herself together.

"Nial, please tell me what ye believe is happenin'," she asked softly.

"I do no' believe yer da, or Duncan, are traitors. There must be a reason why they would make such admissions. I can only assume it has something to do with the fact that Isobel and Aishlinn are missin'." He took a deep breath and turned to face his wife.

Bree's beautiful green eyes were missing their usual sparkle. They were filled with worry and questions Nial could not answer.

"I want ye to take Jamie and go to Findley and Maggy's," Nial told her. He stopped her before she could protest. "Bree, within the hour I will be leavin' with Caelen for Edinburgh. I canna help Angus or Duncan if I must worry over ye. If me guess is right, someone has Isobel and Aishlinn and are usin' them against Angus and Duncan. I canna let anyone get to ye and Jamie." His voice was soft, yet firm. If he had to tie her up and drag her to Maggy and Findley's, he would.

Nial could see his wife contemplating his argument. After a time, she finally nodded her head in agreement. "I suppose yer right," she said. Maggy and Findley's home was much closer to Stirling than the McKee keep and from there, she might be able to do more to help her parents and rest of her family. But she kept that line of thinking to herself. If Nial caught even an inkling of what she might be thinking, he would probably tie her up and put a dozen guards around her.

Nial breathed a sigh of relief and caressed his wife's cheek before giving her a tender kiss on her forehead. "I will send Ellen up to help ye pack. I've men readying themselves to take ye to Maggy's. If ye leave soon, ye can be in Stirling within three days.

Bree smiled up at her husband and gave his hand a gentle squeeze. "When are they set to hang?" she asked over the lump in her throat.

"If our information is correct, they're plannin' on takin' them to Stirling fer the hangin'. I'm told they'll be leavin' Edinburgh in five days' time. Hopefully, we can figure out what the bloody hell has happened before then and get this all sorted out."

"Has anyone talked to Robert? Has anyone appealed to him?" Bree asked. If anyone could stop her father and Duncan from hanging, it was Robert Stewart, High Steward of Scotland. With King David's capture by the English at Neville's Cross, Robert Steward was leading their country. Bree knew he was the one and only man at the moment who could help her father and Duncan.

"I dunnae. I've only just been told of what happened. I'll ken more when we get to Edinburgh. I believe Wee William is now on his way to get an audience with Robert Stewart as we speak."

THREE

Rowan Graham did not wish to leave his wife, not for any length of time. Kate had grown frail, and depressed after having suffered three miscarriages in the past year. It was beginning to seem impossible for Kate to get beyond her third month. The loss of the babes they so desperately wanted was not only taking its toll on his lovely wife's body, it was killing her spirit. Rowan felt that he lost a little more of Kate each time she lost another babe.

Rowan wanted to stop all attempts, but Kate was insistent. He did not want to lose his wife, for he adored her. Even though theirs was an arranged marriage, it had not taken long before he was hopelessly in love with Kate. The thought of losing her because she tried to give him an heir made him ill.

Try as he might to convince her he would rather go his whole life without any children than to spend a moment of it without her, it was of no use. His words fell on obstinate, stubborn and deaf ears. Kate tried to pretend that she was healthy, hail, and hearty. But Rowan saw the subtle changes in her body and her disposition. Ever vivacious, outgoing, and easy with her laughter and smile, his Kate was growing quieter and she seemed to have far less energy than when they first married.

So when word came that Angus and Duncan were in trouble, Rowan was torn. It had only been a week since Kate's last miscarriage and he wanted to see her fully recovered before even considering leaving her for any reason. But he had fostered with the MacDougalls for ten years and he loved Angus as much as he loved his real father. And Duncan was the closest thing to a brother that he had.

Should he stay and see that Kate took care of herself or go to the aid of his foster father and brother? He anguished over the decision. He did not want to leave his wife. But how could he say no to Angus or Duncan or to the Bond of The Seven Clans?

The bond was an important one. Forged between the MacDougalls and Grahams as well as the clans McKee, McDunnah, Lindsay, Randolph and Carruthers two years ago, he could not very well ignore it. It had taken years of hard work on the part of Angus and Andrew, Rowan's father, to achieve the peace and friendship the bond afforded all of them. The bond was a promise to stand together against the English or in any other times of trouble.

Being sentenced to hang for crimes Rowan was quite certain were untrue seemed to be about as dire a circumstance as any. Angus and Duncan needed him. Still, he was quite torn. He could send his father to act as diplomat, but lately, his father had not been faring all that well. Andrew was not much aulder than Angus, but the past months had not been kind to him. Andrew was loathe to admit it, but Rowan could see it plain enough.

In the end, it was Kate who made the decision for him.

"Ye must go," Kate insisted as she rolled her eyes, openly annoyed with her husband.

"And *ye* need to rest," Rowan told her as he adjusted her pillows and fussed with tucking in her blankets. He was doing his best to make her comfortable as if doing so would rid him of some of the guilt he felt.

"What I need is fer ye to stop fussing over *me,* and go help Angus and Duncan," she told him as she leaned back against the pillows. "I am no' an invalid, husband. I will be fine verra soon."

"I canna leave ye, Kate," he said as he smoothed out the wrinkles of her blanket.

"Fer heaven's sake, Rowan!" Kate exclaimed. "Ye are actin' a fool. Do I need to send fer yer mum?"

The mention of his mother sent an involuntary shudder throughout his body.

He knew he was a grown man, a warrior, a husband, and, if his wife had anything to say about it, someday a father. He had fought against the English -- and a few Scots -- in many a battle. On the battlefield, he had no fear and would go against any man when the need arose.

Those were all much easier to battle against than his mum. Enndolynn Graham was a force of nature and not one to be toyed with. She was one of the few people on this earth that he was actually fearful of and that was a fact that his mother used to her full advantage. His mum and dad lived on the other side of the keep from Rowan and Kate and he tried to avoid his mother whenever possible.

His father made threats every other day to give up his the chiefdom and let Rowan take the reins. Rowan had a sneaky suspicion however, that his mother would not allow it. She enjoyed being the chatelaine of the keep far too much to give it up. Not even to Kate, who was probably the only living human being that Enndolynn loved unconditionally.

Much to his consternation, Kate and Enndolynn were good friends. Though he could not understand *why* or *how.* Kate had a sweet and sunny disposition. She was eager to help those in need, had a soft spot in her heart for all animals, even mice, and everyone adored her. He could not say the same of his mum.

As Rowan raised an eyebrow he saw a determined look come over wife's face. It was no idle threat that Kate made. He could see the determination in her beautiful green eyes.

"Ye wouldna dare," he said, though he had no doubt that she would.

Kate rolled her eyes again. "I would," she told him. Her lips pursed for a moment before relaxing into that sweet smile that melted his heart every time she offered it to him.

Mayhap were she not such a beautiful young woman, full of sweetness, light and love, he might have stood a better chance against her when she had her mind set on something. He was a hopeless fool when it came to telling her no. He realized early on in their marriage, that it was her smile more than anything else that did him in. He couldn't bear to see it leave her lovely face.

"Rowan," she said softly as she took his hand in hers. He scooted the stool a bit closer to the bed and leaned in. "Husband, I will be fine. Yer mum is here to look after me. She'll no' allow anything to happen to me."

He knew that to be true. His mother adored Kate and there was nothing she would not do to ensure Kate's safety and well-being. If Rowan had to leave, there was some comfort in knowing that Enndolynn would fight the devil himself if she had to in order to protect Kate.

Even with the knowledge that his mother was here to see to his wife's every need, it was not the same as him being there for her.

Apparently Kate could tell that Rowan was mulling things over in his mind, not quite ready yet to agree to leave. "Rowan, ye'll only be gone a week or two. By the time ye return, I'll be well and rested and back on my feet. Besides, the way ye fuss over me makes it harder to rest!"

She would not give in. He decided it was better to give in than to argue. Inevitably she would win. He let out a heavy sigh of defeat, gave her hand a gentle squeeze and leaned over to kiss her forehead. "Ye are a stubborn lass, Kate."

Her face lit with a proud smile. "Yer mum taught me well," she teased.

Rowan scowled down at her, disgusted with the thought. "Ye are *nothin'* like me mum." The comparison was laughable.

Kate giggled softly. "Oh, don't be so daft! Really, Rowan, I do no' ken why yer so afraid of yer mum!"

"I am no' afraid of her." They both knew that to be a lie. "She just sets me teeth on edge."

Kate giggled again as she looked up at her husband. She rested her palm against his cheek and sighed contentedly. "Yer a good man, Rowan Graham. Now go, help Angus and Duncan. They need ye more than I do."

"I'll only go if ye promise ye'll no' leave this bed until I return," he told her.

A devious smile came to her face. "As long as ye promise ye'll no' leave it after ye return. At least not fer a sennight."

He returned her smile. "Yer a wicked woman, Kate!"

"Aye. *That* I learned from ye!"

Rowan wiggled his eyebrows, kissed her soundly on her lips and left the room before he could change his mind.

FOUR

It was difficult for Wee William to maintain any semblance of composure. The looks of disdain and reproach he had received from the people at Castle Stirling were, he supposed, to be expected considering the condition he and Black Richard were in when they presented themselves. Covered with mud and muck -- and God only knew what else -- they looked more like beggars than warriors and probably smelled far worse.

It also did not help matters that Wee William stood nearly seven feet tall. Life had taught him early on that people took one look at his size and stature and assumed him to be an uneducated dullard of a man. Those assumptions usually worked to Wee William's advantage and to the detriment of the fools who made them.

Wee William and Black Richard, along with fifty other MacDougall warriors, had ridden nearly nonstop for days to reach Castle Stirling. To be dismissed so easily by the people there was beyond the pale. They had made it past the guards at the gate, only to be met by an arrogant, thin man who informed them that Robert Stewart was not in residence. He refused to tell Wee William or Black Richard where the High Steward of Scotland might be.

Robert Stewart was the only man in Scotland at the moment that could help. With King David held prisoner by the English, Robert Stewart had been made the High Steward of Scotland. He was the only man who could nullify the death sentences issued for Angus and Duncan.

What set Wee William's teeth to grinding was the thin man's indifference and lack of concern. No matter how they presented the facts he would not budge from his determination not to disclose the whereabouts of the High Steward. He sniffed condescendingly before having guards escort Wee William and Richard off the premises.

Selfishly, Wee William wished his beautiful wife, Nora, were here with him. She was one of the few people who could temper his anger, calm his wrath and sooth away his worries. She was, however, back at their cottage on MacDougall lands tending to their children -- twins, William John and Suisan Elise, and his young brother- and sister-in-law, John and Elise.

God willing, he would be home within a few weeks. He wanted nothing more than to wrap his arms around her wee frame, kiss her soundly and, mayhap, continue to work on producing a few more bairns.

He missed his home, his wife, and their family.

Forcing himself back to the here and now, Wee William stood in disbelief just outside the gates of Stirling Castle. He had to remind himself that laying siege to the castle would serve no benefit to anyone, least of all Angus and Duncan.

But something niggled at him, made the hairs on his neck and arms stand at full attention. Something was amiss. His gut told him that he had been lied to and that Robert Stewart was somewhere within the castle walls, though why the man refused to see him was perplexing. Angus had always considered Robert an ally as well as a friend. Wee William could not understand why Robert would turn his back on his friend in his time of need.

"Wee William." It was Black Richard's voice that broke his train of thought. "Do ye believe them when they say the Stewart is no' here?"

Wee William shook his head as he continued to stare up at the castle. "Nay," he answered. "He's there. I can feel it in me bones."

"Why do ye suppose he refused to see us?"

While Wee William's family needed him to return, Angus and their clan needed him to succeed in meeting with Robert Stewart. If he failed at the latter, he stood the risk of losing more than his home. If Angus and Duncan died, there would be nothing to stop the Stewart from taking control of Clan MacDougall. He could install anyone he wished as chief and there was no guarantee that Angus' replacement would come from within the clan. The thought of a complete stranger as chief of his clan chilled Wee William to the marrow.

A plan suddenly emerged in Wee William's mind. Aye, it would be risky and could very well mean he would hang alongside Angus and Duncan. But it was a chance he was willing to take.

"Well, Black Richard," Wee William began as he finally turned toward his friend. "What say we go and ask the man himself?"

"And how do ye plan on askin' him that question?" Black Richard's brow furrowed over his deep blue eyes.

Wee William gave him a smile and a slap on the back as they turned to walk away from the castle. Black Richard looked like a wee lad as he walked next to his friend. There were times, such as now, when the twinkle of something sinister and devious alight in Wee William's eyes made Black Richard very glad to have the man on his side.

"To his face, me friend."

Black Richard studied Wee William from the corner of his eye, waiting patiently for his friend to explain. Wee William was smiling and did not look nearly as deflated or angry as he had just moments ago. *Oh, this will no' bode well for any of us, least of all for the people inside the castle.*

As Black Richard figured out what Wee William meant to do, he could not help but smile.

"Ye be a devious bastard, Wee William,"

"So I've been told."

FIVE

"Ye've been a good wife to me, lass." Carlich Lindsay's voice was low and scratchy as he spoke to his beautiful young wife. "Had I met ye in me younger days, I would have given ye at least ten bairns." He managed to smile, though in truth he was in a good deal of pain. Dying was not as easy as he would have liked.

He wished the Good Lord would take him soon.

"Wheest, now," his wife said with a shake of her head as she wiped his sweaty brow with a cool cloth.

"Nay, I will no' *wheest*," he told her. "There is much I need to tell ye."

"Ye need to rest, my laird," she whispered as she turned her ministrations to his hands, masking her worry behind a gentle smile. Carlich was auld, very auld, and he'd been on a downward slide toward death for months now.

Wrinkled and sagging skin, seemingly translucent with its bluish tint, hung from his bones. Age and disease were taking their toll on this once strong, virile man.

Arline had not known him back then, when he was young, so full of life and strength. Nay, she'd only known him in his auld age. A twinge of regret played around her heart. She too wished they could have married at a different time. She imagined he *would* have given her as many bairns as she wanted.

Arline had turned five and ten but a month before she and Carlich were married. He was auld enough to be her great-grandsire. Now, three years later, he was more than eighty, and there would be no more bairns for him. And none for her.

"I'll be resting soon enough, fer a verra long time," Carlich said, wheezing.

Lady Arline decided it would do no good to argue .He was auld, frail, and at death's door. There was no fighting the inevitable and to prolong it seemed inhumane. Still, she wanted to make him as comfortable as possible and she was not quite ready to say goodbye. Selfishly, she wished he could live a few more years for when he did die, she knew she would be sent back to Ireland. There were many things she longed for and missed about her homeland. But Ireland was where her father was and he was the sole reason she had no desire to return.

"Fine," she said softly. "I'll allow ye to tell me what is so important. But then, please, husband, I beg ye to rest." She loved him. She loved him because he was good to her and had kept her safe these past three years.

She had learned much from him. He had allowed her the freedom she hadn't realized she had longed for. Arline was allowed to smile, to laugh, to be straightforward with him. Whatever happened to be on her mind at any given time, she was freely allowed to express. Carlich had taught her that the only stupid question was the one not asked.

He had treated her like a precious granddaughter, spoiling her with gifts and freedom. She thrived here and reveled in the sparkle she could bring to his eyes.

How could she not spoil him in return?

Carlich raised an eyebrow. "Ye'll allow it?" he asked mischievously. His tone of voice and raised eyebrow made Arline giggle.

"Aye," she said firmly. "I'll *allow* it." She could not resist the urge to smile when she saw the much-missed twinkle return to his eyes.

SIX

The rain was relentless. It pelted down like small stones on the three hundred MacDougall men as they rode toward the Lindsay keep. The wind was just as unforgiving as the rain as it blew mightily across the wide valley. Brothers Daniel and David led the way across the Lindsay lands, ignoring the assault Mother Nature was heaping upon them.

Weather such as this was nothing new for these strong, fierce and determined men. What made it unusual was the fact that it had been rainy, cold, and windy for nearly a fortnight. It was if the earth itself felt the pall that had been cast across the Highlands with the accusations made against Angus McKenna.

Angus had been the chief of Clan MacDougall longer than Daniel and David had been alive. The two young men loved Angus as much as they loved their own father. To have such charges made against their chief was the same as casting aspersions against their own father and themselves. They could not and would not tolerate such malevolent accusations.

It mattered not to Daniel or David, or to the men traveling with them, that Angus and Duncan had admitted guilt. Not a one of them believed either man was a traitor. In their heart of hearts they knew there had to be a reason for Angus and Duncan to admit to such atrocities. The fact that Isobel, Aishlinn and the babes were missing had to be the key. The two men had admitted guilt in order to protect their families. Nothing else made any sense. They would lend no credence to the accusations or the subsequent admissions. To do so was unthinkable.

The MacDougall warriors had ridden nearly non-stop for two days. They had plodded through thick mud, forded large streams filled with bone-chilling water and ridden around mountains to get to the Lindsay keep.

They had to speak with the chief of the Lindsay clan, Seamus Lindsay. Angus and Duncan were imprisoned in Edinburgh. Without knowing the whys or the wherefores behind the accusations and admissions or the whereabouts of Isobel and Aishlinn, MacDougall warriors had been dispersed across Scotland to invoke the bond of the seven.

The MacDougall Clan council had voted to install Wee William as temporary chief until the mess with Angus and Duncan could be sorted out. Wee William had sent Daniel and David and some three hundred men to the Lindsays. Black Richard went with Wee William and fifty men to Stirling while a contingent of some one hundred MacDougall warriors was sent with Caelen McDunnah to seek help from Nial McKee. Still others had been sent to the clans Randolph and Carruthers.

The orders given to Daniel and David were simple. Get to the Lindsays, invoke the bonds and promises forged between the seven clans, and take Seamus and his men to Stirling. They could not afford any delay in their duty. Angus and Duncan's lives were at risk.

They tore hell-bent-for-leather through the countryside, men on a mission, unstoppable. Failure was not an option.

The MacDougall warriors had been on Lindsay land for more than three hours and had yet to see even a hint of a Lindsay warrior. Typically, scouts were posted along the clan borders to guard them and keep out any unwanted individuals.

Odd. *Very* odd. The lack of soldiers left a rather unsettled feeling in the pit of Daniel's stomach. It was highly unusual.

"If I didna know better, brother," David said, "I'd believe the Lindsays had fallen off the face of the earth."

Daniel nodded and pulled his horse to a halt in order to scan their surroundings. Mayhap the Lindsays were in some kind of trouble and the MacDougalls were heading into a trap.

"Pull ten, no, twenty men, David, and send them ahead," Daniel ordered. "Have them go quickly, but let them no' be seen. I want to ken what the bloody hell is going on, but I do no' want to lose any men."

David gave a quick nod and turned his horse away. In short order, he had twenty good men pulled from the ranks and sent on their way toward the Lindsay keep.

"Do we wait here, Daniel, until the scouts return?" David asked as he shifted in his saddle. Although he loved riding as much as any other man, his arse had gone numb. He could not wait to be off his horse, to stretch his legs, and mayhap enjoy a hot bath and a good meal. But such creature comforts would have to wait.

Daniel thought on David's question for a moment before answering. "Nay, we forge on to the Lindsay keep. We'll slow the pace a bit for now, but we must get to Seamus as soon as possible."

David gave another nod, adjusting the hood of his cloak as he urged his horse onward. The men did not wait for instructions, wordlessly falling in behind their leaders.

Three hours later, the rain had gone from its torrential offensive to a slightly softer splatter and the wind had settled but the sky was still a dark, iron gray. It was an improvement, albeit a small one.

They were just under a mile from the Lindsay keep when Daniel and David caught up with the scouts.

"Their towers are manned, Daniel," a young soldier informed him. "Their flags still fly. It does no' appear anything is amiss."

Custom dictated that flags were withdrawn whenever the chief or leader of a clan was away from his keep for any extended period. If the flags were flying it meant that Seamus was in the keep. Why the Lindsays had no scouts along the boarders or this close to their keep was anyone's guess.

Daniel chewed on the inside of his cheek as he thought on the situation for a few moments. There were two reasons why no scouts patrolled the Lindsay borders. One, there *was* trouble afoot and the MacDougalls could be riding into it. Or two, it could be that Seamus had already learned what had happened to Angus and Duncan and he and his men had readied themselves and now waited for instructions. Something warned Daniel that it was not the latter.

"David, stay back with half our men. I'll take the others on to the keep. Mayhap Seamus has already learned the news and he has left for Edinburgh. Or he and his men await us inside the walls of the keep," Daniel said as he rolled his head in a circle to work the kinks out of his neck. "I still do no' like the fact that no one greeted us at the border."

"I agree. Me gut warns me somethin' be no' right. I can feel it in me bones as well."

"If all be well, I'll send someone back fer ye," Daniel said before giving instructions for half the men follow him.

"Keep a vigilant watch, little brother," Daniel said with a smile before guiding his horse away. "I do no' wish to tell mum that I lost ye."

David laughed aloud and called back to his brother. "Aye, she would miss me more than ye, fer I be her favorite child!"

They both knew it was a lie. It was their baby sister, Moira, who was their mother's favorite child, and everyone knew it. She was, after all, the only daughter among seven sons. Though their mum would deny having a favorite child, each of the brothers knew it to be true. Moira was the sweet, bonny lass every mum dreamed of having for a daughter. It only made sense that she would hold a very special place in their mum's heart. The sons of Floyd of Dunshire were, after all, hell-raising, woman-chasing, fight-seeking men.

Although their mum and sister were sorely outnumbered by the men in their family, all knew 'twas the women who were in charge. They had the sons of Floyd wrapped securely around their dainty little fingers. Neither Daniel, David nor any of their five brothers would have it any other way.

Daniel and his band of MacDougall men took great care in arriving at the gates of the Lindsay keep. Vigilant and watchful, their keen senses were on high alert and their weapons were at the ready. The closer they drew to the keep, the more Daniel's instincts warned him something was amiss. That warning pulled tightly in his gut, his eyes open for the slightest irregular movement ahead of them, his ears keenly alert for the slightest sound of trouble.

They passed several cottages that sat near the walls of the keep. Smoke billowed from chimneys, battling with the breeze and the rain. Furs covered the windows and doors were pulled shut. Daniel supposed the rain could be what kept people in doors.

Daniel and his men were able to ride straight to the gates of the keep, without so much as a how-do-ye-do from anyone. The three-story Lindsay keep was old, but in good repair. Constructed of large blocks of limestone, it had a tall, thick curtain wall surrounding it. Not quite as big as the Clan MacDougall keep, it was still a formidable site.

The scouts had been correct. Nothing appeared amiss. The Lindsay flags were raised. Drenched from all the rain, they hung limply from their staffs. Occasionally, a gust of wind would catch the heavy fabric and beat it against the wooded poles. Save for the thud and whack of the sodden flags, an eerie silence enveloped the keep.

"Who goes there?" a man shouted from atop the wall, breaking the unnerving silence. The sound startled Daniel's horse, which whinnied its protest before angrily shaking its head. Daniel shushed the animal and patted its neck, quickly settling the animal.

Daniel could barely make out the shapes of men along the upper wall. The disembodied voice sounded auld and tired. He sat taller in his saddle, one hand holding the reins, the other resting on the hilt of his sword. "I be Daniel, of the Clan MacDougall," he shouted into the rain and wind. "We need to meet with Seamus Lindsay. It is a matter of utmost importance."

Daniel and his men kept a safe distance from the gate, should the need to defend themselves arise. From his vantage point, he could see along the upper wall and the upper stories of the keep. He could make out three dark shadows along the wall, the fact that set his nerves on alert. There should be at least a dozen men lining those walls.

"And what business do ye have with the Lindsay?" the voice called out. Daniel was finally able to make out which shadow the voice belonged to. He wore a long black cloak with the hood pulled over his head. The man resembled more a hangman than a watchman. Daniel hoped that was not a sign of things to come.

Daniel gritted his teeth before he answered. "We come on urgent business that is fer Seamus' ears alone. Tell him that Angus McKenna, chief of the Clan MacDougall, is invoking the bond and promises of the seven. He'll ken what that means."

The figure stood still as stone, as if he were sizing up the matter.

Moments later, he turned and swiftly walked away. A much smaller figure stepped forward. Either a very short man or a young lad had just taken his place.

What the bloody hell is going on with the Lindsays, Daniel wondered. He cast a curious glance at the two soldiers mounted on either side of him. They looked as perplexed and as concerned as Daniel.

Arline sat quietly next to her husband, wholly dumfounded by the information he had just shared. In her right hand, she clutched a small iron key, in her left, her husband's cold, clammy hand.

She felt as though she had just been tossed into an icy loch. Trepidation fell around her like freezing water, sending prickling sensations over her skin. She shuddered, awash in a sea of disbelief. For the first time in a very long time, she felt exceedingly afraid and alone.

Arline stared down at her husband. It had been difficult for him to share these horrid secrets with her. His voice had cracked several times over the past hour as he choked back tears of guilt and remorse.

Although his body had been ravaged by age, the same could not be said of his mind. In complete control of his faculties, he was as lucid and as sharp as anyone she knew.

Were it not for the other person in the room -- the stranger who had arrived less than two hours ago -- Arline would have been content to believe her husband had suffered an apoplexy. However, the stranger hiding in the shadows had shattered that hope by affirming everything Carlich had told her.

"Carlich," she whispered, "Are ye certain?" The information he had just given her would destroy countless lives. Part of her wished she were back in Ireland, but her father was there. Nay, even with Scotland in turmoil and balanced precariously on the cusp of something horrible, it was still better than being anywhere near her father.

Carlich nodded his head and gave her hand a gentle squeeze. "Aye, lass, I be certain. Do as I told ye. Keep that key and the box with ye at all times. I need ye to leave straight away for Stirling."

Her heart pounded ferociously. "But husband, why me? Mayhap *he* should do this," Arline said with a nod toward the silent stranger. She was unable to see the man's face for he had not moved from the darkness of the corner.

"He canna do it, wife. Were anyone to ken he was here, we would be as good as dead," Carlich answered. He took a fortifying breath before going on. "Wife, there be no other I can trust."

Carlich knew he was asking much of his wife. She was young and innocent, but he also knew she was a strong and intelligent young woman. He knew she worried over leaving him.

"Wife, I promise I'll no' die until ye return," he said, trying to interject some levity into the serious atmosphere that had taken hold in the room.

Arline was about to chastise him for making light of such a serious matter when a knock came at the bedchamber door. The man in the shadows moved swiftly yet silently toward the door, doing his best to remain in the shadows. He advised Arline to keep his presence secret.

Arline felt uneasy, not liking the clandestine atmosphere that had taken over her home these past few days. And she especially did not like the fact that she could not see the shadow's face. Neither the shadow nor her husband would divulge his identity. It was for her own good they had assured her -- she was better off not knowing.

"M'lady." It was Fergus' voice she heard coming from the other side. At one time, Fergus had been Carlich's second in command. He was younger than Carlich by eight years. Though he was still of sound mind and body, he was far too auld to do more than offer advice and occasionally take a spot on the wall. When he wasn't keeping Carlich engaged he could often be found helping to tend the gardens.

Arline had done her best to convince her husband to share with Fergus what Carlich had shared with her. Carlich refused insisting that the fewer people who were aware, the better off they all were.

Arline stood, tucked the key into the pocket of her dress and hid the box under Carlich's blanket. The stranger gave a nod of his head as he pressed himself further against the wall. Arline resisted the urge to roll her eyes at him before she opened the door just a crack.

"M'lady," Fergus said.

Arline saw the look of apprehension painted on the man's face. *What more could go wrong this day?* She wondered to herself.

"What is wrong, Fergus?" she asked, stepping into the hallway and closing the door behind her.

"There be men at the gate. At least a hundred. They be MacDougalls."

Arline's brow knitted as she waited for Fergus to catch his breath and continue.

"They say they need to speak with Seamus. He said to say that Angus McKenna sent them and he wishes to invoke the bond and promise of the seven."

That bit of news, combined with what Carlich had just told her, sent another involuntary shiver down Arline's spine. She knew exactly what those words meant, for Carlich had shared it in confidence with her not long ago.

Seven clans had formed an alliance. They would work together to fight for Scotland's freedom against the English, or any other invaders. And should any one of the seven clans invoke the bond, the others would respond with whatever aid they could.

When Carlich had divulged what he knew of the meeting, Arline had been surprised. She had asked him how he knew of the secret meetings. Carlich simply smiled and waggled his eyebrows. "People have a habit of speakin' freely among the verra auld and the verra young. Mayhap because they think the verra auld or the verra young incapable of understandin' certain things."

"Verra well," Arline muttered. "Allow only three to enter. Take them to Carlich's auld study. Have a fire lit and food brought to them. I shall meet with them shortly."

Fergus put forth no effort to disguise his surprise. "Ye, m'lady?" he asked.

"Well, ye dunna think Carlich can meet with them, do ye? Or mayhap I should ask the cook or the stable master to go in my stead?"

Were it anyone else Arline that had spoken to in that tone, they would have run away with their tail betwixt their legs. Fergus was not one of those people. He smiled, realizing at once that he had underestimated the determination of his lady.

"Me apologies, lass. I sometimes ferget what a determined young woman ye be."

Arline smiled brightly before shooing him away and returning to her husband's bedside. She did her best to ignore the quiet man in the shadows but 'twas next to impossible. Even hidden in the shadows his countenance bespoke a man of great power, though not necessarily in the physical sense of the word. Nay, it was something else altogether. Instinctively she knew 'twas better to have the man as an ally than an enemy.

Daniel was only slightly relieved when they were granted permission to enter. He was very curious to find out where the rest of the Lindsay men were. He chose Ronald and Roy to accompany him into the keep. The rest of his men would make a temporary camp just outside the keep's walls.

As soon as they walked through the open gates two young lads came to tend to their horses. Daniel and his men were taken to the keep, led by a man of questionable age. The auld man had introduced himself as Fergus before telling them to follow him.

With their clothes and boots drenched, Daniel and his men left a trail of water along the stone floor of the keep. There was no way around it other than stripping to bare skin and leaving the sodden clothes at the door. Daniel reckoned that none of the women of the keep would appreciate such obnoxious behavior.

The auld man, Fergus, took them to the second floor of the keep. No warriors, no young men capable of defending the keep were seen as they walked down a long, dark corridor. Only women and children seemed to grace the rooms and hallways.

The room to which Fergus took Daniel and his men smelled of age and dust, as if it hadn't been used in a goodly number of years. A fire roared in the fireplace, its warmth immediately drawing Daniel and his men toward it. The warmth from the crackling flames felt good against their cold, damp skin. Without a word, Fergus left them to their own devices, quietly closing the door behind him.

The men, soaked and cold to their bones, peeled off their plaids, draping the sodden fabric over the backs of chairs set next to the fire. They were left standing in damp tunics, trews and boots.

As they stood warming themselves by the fire, a young woman entered the room carrying a tray filled with tankards of ale. Following close behind her was an older woman with a tray of cheeses, breads, and meats. Neither woman spoke as she set her tray on the dusty table near the tall windows. Daniel guessed the younger lass to be around six and ten, the older woman as old as Methuselah.

The pretty lass smiled and curtsied at the young men, but cast a flirtatious wink toward Ronald. The auld woman gave a haughty, disapproving humph as she pulled the young girl from the room. As the door closed, Daniel heard the auld woman chastising the young girl. "Them be MacDougall *men*, lassie! Ye want nothin' to do with that lot. Womanizers every one of them be."

The three MacDougall men in question eyed each other for a moment before bursting into laughter. "I see our reputation precedes us," Ronald said.

Daniel and Roy agreed.

"I do no' think of meself as a womanizer," Daniel said. "More of a teacher of the ways of the heart."

"More like ways of the body," Roy said with a snort.

It felt good to laugh, even for a brief moment. They were also thankful to be out of the rain and wind, even if the reprieve was temporary.

They assumed that Seamus would be along shortly and soon, they would be back on the road for Stirling. Holding trenchers of food, they sat in the chairs in front of the fire, soaking up the heat, enjoying the quiet solitude that settled in around them.

Little did they know as they warmed themselves that it would be a long time before they laid eyes on Seamus Lindsay.

SEVEN

Word of Angus and Duncan's incarceration had spread across the Highlands like wild fire. By the time Caelen and Nial and Bree and their son had arrived at Findley and Maggy McKenna's palatial estate, Findley had his men at the ready.

Nial's original plan had been to send Bree and Jamie ahead with a handful of men while he and Caelen rode on to Edinburgh. Caelen disagreed, raising concern over the fact that they still had no idea where Isobel and Aishlinn were. There was nothing to say that whoever had taken the two women and the children weren't also preparing to take the rest of Angus' family.

Nial considered that prospect and agreed. Admittedly, he was relieved as well as happy to spend another few days with his wife and babe.

Before leaving the McKee keep, Nial sent word to Bridgett, Angus and Isobel's adopted daughter. She lived in Ireland with her husband, Timothy, and their four children. Nial wasn't taking any chances with losing more of Angus' family. Though it would take weeks for his men to reach the tiny village where Bridgett and her family lived, he felt it made sense to warn them of the situation.

Nial could only hope there would be a happy outcome to this mess. He dreaded the thought of sending word to Bridgett that her father and brother were dead.

While Findley and Maggy had been expecting Caelen and Nial and their men, they were not prepared for Bree and her babe. They had been standing at the top of the steps that led into their home when they caught sight of Bree and little Jamie. After exchanging confused glances with one another, Findley and Maggy welcomed their friends with open arms, careful not to show the concern each of them felt. Both had similar lines of thought: *If Bree and Jamie are here, then things are far worse than we thought.*

Bree had been perched atop her husband's lap, with Jamie wrapped in her arms for most of the ride. The damp air and biting wind made it feel more like late winter than summertime. Nial draped a heavy fur around his wife and babe, shielding them from the harsh weather. He was quite proud of his son, even though he was just a bairn. Jamie had been very little trouble on the journey. Kept fed and dry, he was perfectly content in his mother's arms.

Nial guided his horse toward the steps of the keep. Stable boys appeared immediately to tend to their horses. Findley bounded down the steps and handed Jamie off to Maggy before helping Bree down. In no time, the family was ushered into the warm and dry keep.

"We were no' expecting ye, Bree!" Maggy exclaimed as she led them into the large gathering room.

Bree was exhausted, but not so much that she couldn't take notice of the opulent surroundings. Maggy's home was filled with fine, ornately carved furniture. Beautiful paintings and tapestries hung on nearly every wall. Three heavy iron chandeliers filled with too many candles to count hung from the beamed ceiling. Instead of rushes covering the wood floor, dozens of finely crafted rugs were scattered about. Bree imagined they could have fit four, mayhap five of her homes inside this beautiful castle.

"Och!" Maggy said as Bree pulled down the hood of her heavy cloak. "Lass, yer soaked to the bone!" She was still holding Jamie, bouncing from one leg to the other as she kissed his soft cheeks.

Bree laughed. "Aye, we did no' stop much and neither did the rain."

"We'll get ye settled into a warm room above stairs. We'll get ye all baths and food, and ye can tell me what the devil is happenin' with yer da and family."

Before Bree could explain that she knew very little, Nial was at her side. He rested a hand on her waist and gave her a kiss on her cheek.

Bree smiled but remained quiet as they were all led above stairs. She wanted to get out of her wet clothes and into a hot bath. As bone tired and cold as she felt, she thought it might be a day or two before she felt warm again. She wished she could climb into a soft, warm bed with Nial's arms wrapped around her and forget about the rest of the world.

Then she thought of her father and Duncan.

The image of them sitting in a dungeon in Edinburgh was the one thing that kept her moving one foot determinedly in front of the other. In the beginning of this journey, anger over the accusations had boiled her blood enough to help keep the chill away. But now, the anger had turned to worry and it was difficult to keep a positive outlook or to remain hopeful.

I am the daughter of Angus and Isobel, Bree thought as she slipped behind a dressing screen and stripped out of her wet clothes. When she tossed her dress across the top of the screen, it nearly toppled over. Maggy, still holding Jamie, offered her a heavy blanket before turning her attention back to the cooing babe.

"He's a beautiful lad," Maggy offered as she gently bounced the babe in her arms. "If he is as calm as his da is, I think he'd suit me Deirdre. She already has me temper. She'll need a good, calm man to keep her in check."

Bree smiled slightly as she sat in a chair next to the fire. "Sometimes I wish his da was no' so calm," Bree admitted.

Maggy looked up from the babe and smiled warmly at Bree. "Aye, I suppose so. I'd wager that ye be wantin' him to race to Edinburgh and lay siege to the whole town so that he can get yer da and Duncan out of this mess."

Bree nodded her head and fought back the tears. "I ken it sounds foolish, but aye, that is what I wish we could do."

Jamie started to fuss and suck on his fist. "I think he's hungry," Maggy offered as she placed the babe in Bree's arms.

Bree opened the blanket just enough to give Jamie room to suckle. He latched on quickly and his expression made her chuckle. "As if ye haven't eaten in days," she told him. "Yer da gets that hungry, desperate look in his eyes, too."

Maggy giggled as she pulled a chair up to sit across from Bree. "So it isn't just Findley that does that? Gets the look of a man starved half out of his mind?"

Bree giggled her agreement. "From what Aishlinn and me mum tell me," her voice trailed off at thinking of her parents and family. Her stomach felt heavy, tight, the worry continuing to build.

No matter what her father and Duncan had admitted, she refused to believe them. It simply was not possible.

"Maggy," she said as soft tears made their way down her cheeks. "I ken in me heart that me da is no traitor."

Maggy nodded her head but remained quiet.

"And neither is Duncan. They'd no more betray their country or King David than Nial or Findley would!" Frustration began to wrap its way around her heart. "I do no' care that they've admitted guilt. I can only think they did so because of mum and Aishlinn. No one kens where they be. Mayhap someone has taken them, holds them against their will and is forcing Da and Duncan to do this. 'Tis the only thing that makes any sense."

"Aye, 'tis possible," Maggy said softly. "I do no' ken Angus or Duncan well, but they do no' strike me as traitors. And Findley agrees."

They sat in silence for some time, their eyes absentmindedly transfixed on the suckling babe in Bree's arms. A knock on the door shook the women from their quiet reverie. Maggy bid entry and a moment later three lads entered, with buckets full of hot water.

"Thank ye kindly, lads," Maggy said as they made their way to the tub behind the screen. One by one they emptied the steamy water into the tub before quietly leaving the room.

"Ye'll feel better after a bath and a hot meal," Maggy told Bree as she took the now sleeping Jamie from her arms.

Bree sat still for a moment before shaking her head. "Nay, I'll no' feel better until me da and Duncan are safely out of Edinburgh."

Two hours later, Bree and Maggy kissed their husbands goodbye. Before the men were out of the courtyard, Maggy and Bree began making plans of their own. The men were heading to Edinburgh with the hope they could talk Phillip Lindsay into rescinding the death sentence.

"I'll no' let me father hang fer something I know in me heart he did no' do," Bree said as she paced anxiously across the floor of the bedchamber. "And I ken as well that Duncan would never betray his country," she rambled on, paying very little attention to Maggy.

Maggy said nothing as she sat in a chair next to the fire and nursed her new daughter, Elizabeth. The child suckled contentedly as she held onto Maggy's index finger. The babe looked like her da, as did two-year-old Deirdre. Maggy's five boys were in charge of keeping little Deirdre out of trouble this morning.

Findley was Angus' nephew. His father, Collom McKenna, Angus' younger brother, had been killed in the same massacre that took Duncan McEwan's family. Though Findley was the eldest of the three lads, he had made it known early on that he had no desire to become chief. He preferred, instead, to be warrior.

But life does not always turn out the way one wishes. Findley, through his marriage to Maggy, was now the proud chief of their growing clan. Maggy's first husband, Gawter De Menteith, had been the seventh Earl of Kerse. Blessedly, the pox had taken the hard, cruel man, years earlier.

"I do no' like just *sitting* here, waiting!" Bree was growing angrier as the moments passed by.

Maggy looked up from her daughter and smiled. "Angus and Duncan haven't even left Edinburgh yet."

Suddenly, an idea came to Bree. She stopped in her tracks, spun and looked at Maggy with wide eyes and a smile that began to grow as the idea formed into a full-fledged plan. Her anger and dread were rapidly fading away as hope began to build.

"Maggy," Bree said excitedly. "I have an idea…" her words trailed off and she began to chew on her thumbnail.

Maggy's brows drew inward as she tilted her head. "What *kind* of *idea?*" she asked.

Bree took a quick breath in before answering. "What if Angus and Duncan didna arrive in Stirling at all?"

Bree could almost see the wheels in Maggy's mind begin to turn. "Bree, ye be far more devious than I could have imagined."

Maggy understood, as well as anyone, the lengths to which a mother would go to protect her children. She imagined too, that if Findley were in the same predicament as Angus and Duncan, she would do whatever she could to help him.

"Of course, we'll be needin' help," Maggy said as she looked down at her daughter, who was now content and fast asleep. "Findley took most of the men to Stirling. But, he didna take *all* those that could help us."

Bree's smile grew along with the twinkle in her eyes. For the first time in days she began to feel hopeful. Aye, her husband would probably be very upset with her. In the end, however, she knew he would understand.

's Honor

EIGHT

Twenty-five mounted soldiers surrounded the prison wagon that held Angus McKenna and Duncan McEwan. Ten soldiers led the way down the rutted, winding path to Stirling. The remaining guards were at the rear.

Large puddles of murky water littered the rough road. The trees hung limp, weighed down by the relentless rain. The deep green leaves, the near black tree trunks, the sodden ground and the gloomy sky left the prisoners longing for the comforts of home and hearth.

It was difficult to judge the exact time of day by looking at the sky, for it was as gray as an auld Highlander's beard. Under different circumstances, Angus might have relied on his belly to tell him the time. His stomach had given up growling some days ago and he swore he'd never eat another bowl of gruel again, no matter how long he might or might not live.

Duncan longed to be home with his wife and bairns. *If* by some divine intervention he made it out of this alive -- there was a very good chance that he wouldn't -- he would take a long hot bath and climb into his soft warm bed with Aishlinn. And he would not leave the comfort of that bed or her arms for at least a month.

A light breeze flittered through the bars of the prison wagon, stirring the fetid air. Angus doubted man had yet to create a word that would describe the awful stench that emanated from his body. Sweat and grime blended together to create such a foul smell that it burned his nose and caused his eyes to water. He imagined a roll in horse dung would be an improvement over the revolting way he currently smelled. It was no wonder the soldiers were keeping their distance.

Angus chuckled softly, trying to lighten the mood. "Ye'd think they were transportin' the king himself," he said.

Duncan agreed. "Aye. But I think I'd prefer one of the king's coaches to *this*," he said as he shoved bits of dirty rushes away with his feet.

They were the only passengers -- if one could call them that seeing how they were chained together at their wrists and ankles. Side by side, they sat with their backs against the solid wall of the wagon.

Stale rushes strewn across the floor smelled of urine and vomit. These weren't *worst* living conditions Angus had ever experienced, but it they were close.

They were less than a day's ride from Stirling. Angus calculated that at their current pace, it would be long after nightfall before they arrived at

Stirling Castle.

Although it had been difficult to receive word about his wife, daughter and grandchildren, it had not been impossible. Aye, he knew the bastards who had taken them. Knew them all to well. And the bastards knew that there was nothing Angus would not do for any of them. Arrogantly, the fools believed they had the upper hand. What they did not know however was that Angus' death did not necessarily mean that *they* themselves would succeed. Neither did it mean they would live beyond another fortnight.

The fools took too much for granted, were far too arrogant to see any errors with their plan to see him hang. In the end, it would be their greed, arrogance and stupidity that would seal their fates. Whether Angus hanged or not, it simply didn't matter. They were dead men. They just didn't realize it yet. Chances were they would not see it until the very last moment, right before a sword gutted them or the noose draped around *their* necks. No matter what method of death was eventually chosen, they would die.

Angus took some satisfaction in knowing that fact.

An eerie silence had fallen across the land. The rain had kept the birds, red deer, and other animals in seclusion. The silence was broken only by the sound of the heavy hooves slopping through the mud and muck, the occasional jingle of harness, the creaking of the wagon, and the occasional whisper between Angus and Duncan. It had been some time since the guards had uttered a single word.

Angus wondered how many of the soldiers were enjoying this foray north to Stirling. A few of them refused to look Angus in the eye, either out of shame for his misdeeds or fear of his reputation as a warrior. At the moment, he didn't care what the reasons were for their silence. He was glad to be left alone.

He cast a sideways glance at Duncan. His son-in-law was as good a warrior, man, husband and father as they came. Angus felt guilty for having Duncan involved this mess. He had done everything he could to keep him out of it, but the young man was just as stubborn as Angus.

He had spent days trying to convince Duncan to remain behind and finally take over the role of chief. No matter how Angus tried to convince Duncan that the clan was going to need him as their new chief, Duncan stubbornly refused to listen. Duncan was adamant that Angus needed his help more than the clan did or would.

Duncan had not been a party to everything that had transpired over the past year. In fact, no charges had ever been leveled against him. But when they came to arrest Angus, Duncan had stepped in, like a fool, and had falsely admitted to being involved. Had Angus not already been shackled, he would have beaten some sense into the young man's thick head or at least tried to.

It was too late now to save the man from himself. Duncan knew too much -- not all of it mind you, but enough to be dangerous.

"Do ye think Aishlinn will forgive me?" Duncan asked quietly. He sat with one knee drawn up, a shackled wrist resting on it. His leather trews and once white tunic were covered in dirt and grime and mud splatter. Even with his eyes closed, his face held a solemn expression.

Angus did not need to take any time to think on it. "Aye, she will. Aishlinn is a smart young woman." Angus told him.

"That she is," Duncan readily agreed. "She must get that from her mum."

Angus smiled wanly and nodded his head. Considering where he was at this moment, he had to agree with Duncan's assessment. Were they anywhere but inside a prison wagon, Angus would have taken credit for his daughter's intelligence and tenacity.

"Do ye think they'll ever know *why* we've done what we've done?"

Angus filled his dirty cheeks with air and let it out slowly. "Aye, they will. Eventually," he answered, knowing full well that it would be years before anyone might learn the truth. *Let Duncan hold on to what little hope he had,* Angus thought to himself.

It wasn't supposed to have ended up this way. When he had started on this journey, he had no intentions of ever being hanged as a traitor.

But hang he would, if it meant his people could live in peace.

NINE

Rowan Graham had met up with Nial, Caelen, and Findley in the early morning hours at an inn in Edinburgh. Nial filled his friend in on what he knew, and more importantly, what he didn't know. Rowan reciprocated. They still had no earthly idea where Isobel, Aishlinn and the babes were. The longer they went without knowing, the bigger the knot in Nial's stomach grew.

They decided that Findley would take to the streets of Edinburgh. Rumors often ran amok at times like these and sometimes those rumors held fragments of truth. It might be possible to learn where Isobel and Aishlinn were or some other bit of information that could help Angus and Duncan. While Findley went in search of information, Nial, Caelen and Rowan slept, knowing it could be some time before any of them enjoyed that luxury again.

Annoyed and tired, he returned to the inn just before sunrise. He had learned nothing, a fact that confused and frustrated the men.

While Findley took to his bed for some much needed sleep, Caelen, Rowan and Nial made their way to Phillip Lindsay's home. A lovely young woman, heavy with child, answered the door. The three men assumed she was Phillip Lindsay's housekeeper. After introducing themselves, she curtly dismissed the three of them. No matter how much they begged an audience, she refused them. "Come back after the noonin' meal," she told them firmly just before shutting the door in their faces.

Had they not worried that busting down the door and dragging Phillip Lindsay from his bed would only make matters worse, they would have been far more forceful in their request. But too much was at stake to risk angering one of only two men who could stop the hanging.

The three men returned to the inn, broke their fast, and tried waiting patiently. It was not an easy feat. The longer they sat, the angrier they became and the more their resentment toward Phillip Lindsay grew.

Caelen had grown more than just weary of waiting; he was nearly seething with anger. Calmly, he stood and declared enough was enough. They marched back to Phillip Lindsay's home and this time, they did not ask for permission to see him. As soon as the young woman opened the door, Caelen spoke.

"Lass, we *will* see Phillip *now*. There are lives at stake," Caelen told her.

The young woman had her feet firmly planted, one hand on the door and the other on her hip. "Whose lives?" she demanded to know.

"Phillip Lindsay's if he refuses to see us."

The young woman didn't blink, didn't look fearful or appalled at Caelen's announcement. She rolled her eyes, shook her head and allowed them inside. "Ye wait here." 'Twas an order, not a request.

A quarter hour passed before she returned to take them to Phillip Lindsay's study.

The three men stood before the massive desk belonging to Phillip Lindsay. The rotund man sat hunched over a trencher overflowing with food. He devoured one leg of chicken after another. His fat fingers and lips were covered in grease and bits of chicken clung to both his chins.

They were unmoved by Phillip's insistence that Angus and Duncan were guilty.

"Ye've ken Angus McKenna for twenty years or more," Nial began through gritted teeth. "Ye canna believe the accusations."

Phillip Lindsay sighed heavily and tossed a bare chicken bone onto the trencher. Frustration was etched in his face. His tone was sharp and unforgiving. "I am beginning to get sorely tired of people coming to me to exalt the virtues of Angus McKenna." He cast a disgusted look at both men before continuing. "He's an *admitted* traitor, as is Duncan. I canna help that ye do no' care for the *truth*."

Up to this point, Caelen had remained silent, quietly studying Phillip Lindsay. There was something about the man that Caelen did not like. It could have been his pompous attitude, the disgusting manner in which he ate or the fact that Caelen sensed the man was hiding something.

Caelen took some pride in knowing he could judge a man's character simply by reading his countenance. He had discovered early on in his life that he had been blessed with something of a sixth sense. On more than one occasion, that gift had saved his thick, stubborn head as well as his neck.

"The truth," Caelen said calmly, "is sometimes no' what it seems."

There were different facets of any truth. Or lie for that matter. Similar to the reflections made by a prism. What one saw oftentimes depended on the angle from which one looked. Change the angle and the colors of the prism changed. Sunlight would cast far different colors than the light of a candle.

There may be *some* truth to the accusations, but Caelen did not believe it to be the *whole* truth.

Phillip directed his heated glare at Caelen. "Contrary to what ye might believe, Caelen McDunnah, the charges were no' just grabbed out of the air on a whim."

Caelen's composure remained the same, yet inwardly he was glad that

Phillip finally touched on that particular subject. Caelen preferred a direct approach in most matters. He was done beating around the bush in an attempt to glean some insight as to *why* such charges were leveled against the man he had looked to as another father figure.

"What evidence do ye have?" Rowan asked, beating Caelen to the question.

Phillip eyed the three men speculatively for a moment. "On more than one occasion over the past three years, Angus has been seen in the company of no' one, but *two* English spies," he said before wiping his greasy face clean with the sleeve of his finely brocaded coat. "Ye see, lads, we've spies of our own. And were it no' for Angus McKenna's actions at the Battle of Neville's Cross, our King David would no' have been nearly killed and no' now be a prisoner of the English."

Caelen and Nial cast confused glances at each other. Rowan continued to glare at the man. All of them had fought at Neville's Cross right alongside Angus and Duncan. Many lives had been lost in that battle and King David had nearly died. Their king had been captured that day and was now being held prisoner by the English. These were dark days for all of Scotland.

"I was there, fightin' alongside Angus," Nial seethed. "He fought as brave as any other Scot!"

Phillip leaned back in his chair, shaking his head. "But ye were no' with him every moment of that battle, were ye?"

Nial could not deny that fact. He had been leading his own troops during that fateful battle of last October. Nay, he could not in all honesty say that he could account for Angus' *every* moment. Hope began to dwindle.

"So *yer* spies say they saw Angus with English spies. How do we no' know that Angus was no' workin' *for* us an no' against us? What evidence, besides what yer spies tell ye, do ye have that Angus was workin' for the English?"

"I have Angus' admission of guilt. That is all I need."

Nial began to pace back and forth in front of the large hearth that sat on the opposite side of the room. He only heard half of the exchange between Caelen, Rowan and Phillip. Mulling the situation over in his mind while he paced, he knew spies could not be trusted.

"So yer takin' the word of spies over the word of the most trusted and honorable man any of us in this room has ever known?" Caelen asked.

"Do no' forget that Angus *admitted* to plottin' against the king," Phillip reminded him.

Caelen shook his head slightly. "What *exactly* did Angus admit to?"

Phillip let out a long, heavy sigh before he answered Caelen's question. "To plottin' against the king!" he said, exasperated.

Caelen spread his legs apart and folded his arms across his chest. "Aye, I got that part. Me question is, what *exactly* did he supposedly do to plot against the king?" He was beginning to believe Phillip Lindsay was as dumb as he was pompous. Those two traits could be quite dangerous.

"'Twas Angus who no' only tried to *kill* the king, but when David fled and took refuge under a bridge on River Browney, Angus led the English straight to him!"

Nial stopped pacing and spun, his eyes filled with disgusted astonishment. "Nay! Angus would *never* do such a thing!"

Phillip had grown weary of the conversation. He slapped a palm down hard on the top of his desk. "I would never have believed it meself, ye daft eejits!" he shouted, his temper no longer held in check. He lashed out at the young men. "But Angus admitted to doin' just that! And Duncan admits to helpin' him! And we've witnesses that prove that Angus stabbed David, stabbed him with his own broadsword. Saw it with their own eyes!"

It was all too much for Nial. He took in deep breaths of air and tried to steady his shaking hands. He was sorely tempted to unsheathe his own broadsword and run it through Phillip Lindsay's gut.

"And who be these *witnesses*?" Caelen asked, still unconvinced.

"Me own brother, Seamus Lindsay, and his son, Aric," Phillip said, his voice steady and firm. Nial thought Phillip looked pleased with that answer.

The three men glanced at each other. Nial had paled considerably, no doubt, Caelen assumed, worrying over how he would break this new revelation to Bree. Rowan looked fit to be tied. Seamus Lindsay's reputation as chief of the Lindsay Clan was nearly as stellar as Angus'. If it had been any man *other* than Seamus, Caelen doubted anyone would have believed the accusations, let alone given them enough credence to bring charges.

This revelation put a decisive damper on the hope that something could be done to keep Angus and Duncan from hanging.

"Seamus?" Nial muttered. "Seamus Lindsay says he saw Angus attempt to kill the king? With his own eyes?"

Phillip gave a sideways nod of his head before leaning back in his chair again. "Aye," he said as he rested a plump hand on the top of his desk. "And Aric, his eldest son. They both swear they saw Angus thrust his broadsword into David. Had the man not been so quick on his feet and moved when he did, Angus could have done far more than just pierce his side. He'd have gutted him."

Caelen and Nial were baffled. Nial was trying desperately to cling to some shred of hope that it had all been a terrible mistake. Mayhap Seamus and Aric had only *thought* they saw Angus attempt to gut their king. "Is it possible," Nial asked in a low voice, "that it could have been someone who *looked* like Angus?"

"Aye," Phillip began, sounding as though he were giving some weight to Nial's question. "'Tis possible. 'Tis also possible that the man who stood before my court two days past was no' Angus McKenna but an evil faerie who only *looked* and *sounded* like Angus McKenna. And the young man with him was no' Duncan McEwan, but a possessed brownie also capable of changin' his appearance." When he finished speaking, Philip shook his head, disgusted, and tired of the conversation.

Nial's jaw clenched with Phillip's insults. Had Caelen and Rowan not stopped him, Nial would have lunged over the desk and broken Phillip Lindsay's neck.

Nial, Rowan and Caelen returned to the inn. Nial was angrier than he could ever remember feeling. Frustrated and annoyed, he paced about the small room, cursing Phillip Lindsay's obstinacy and arrogance. It was growing more difficult to keep a lid on his boiling temper.

He worried over his wife and son and how all of this would hurt Bree. She didn't deserve any of this. Silently he swore that if he could, he would find the truth of it all, and strangle the bastard at fault.

Nial's ranting eventually woke Findley. Caelen suggested they go below stairs and get something to eat and drink.

"A few tankards of ale might make ye more tolerable," Caelen told him. "At the very least, it may help me want to strangle ye less." Reluctantly, Nial agreed and the four of them quit the room.

After eating Rowan, Nial and Caelen sat and listened to Findley recount what he had learned during his late night sojourn into the drinking establishments of Edinburgh. Or more importantly, what he hadn't learned.

The fact that he learned nothing spoke volumes. The lack of wagging tongues could only mean one of two things. Either people sincerely did not care, or, they were too afraid to speak on the subject. Findley had to believe it was the latter.

Angus was well known in this part of Scotland, as was Duncan. The MacDougall clan might not be as big as some other clans, but what they lacked in numbers they more than made up for in tenacity, brashness, and bravery. That few people were speaking of the importance of Angus and Duncan being admitted traitors was perplexing.

Those few souls brave enough -- or drunk enough -- to speak on the matter, believed the two men to be guilty. The general vein being that innocent men do not admit to guilt. Hopefully that same line of thinking did not carry to Stirling.

As for Isobel and Aishlinn, their names were never mentioned.

Three sets of eyebrows raised in unison when Findley shared that bit of information with his friends. If in fact the women and children had been taken as a means to force Angus and Duncan into admitting to treason, wouldn't someone somewhere have heard of it? It would take someone with a good deal of power to keep such a thing secret.

Kidnappings, while not an every day occurrence, were a common enough especially in the Highlands. But usually, one knew who took whom and what the ransom demands were before the ink on the ransom letter had dried.

So the four men sat huddled together in a quiet corner of the inn with more questions than answers.

"Someone wants Angus dead," Rowan said as he sipped at his ale.

"But why?" Findley asked to no one in particular.

"Who kens?" Rowan answered. "Angus is no' known fer makin' enemies of anyone other than the English and men of ill repute."

"'Tis true," Nial said. "Most people think more highly of Angus than they do the king."

"That was true, until the events of late, Nial," Rowan said. "But now?" he shook his head as he took another drink.

Nial had no good answer as to why there was the sudden shift in public opinion of his father-in-law. Mayhap, had Angus denied the accusations, those opinions would be quite different. Hordes of people would have come to defend him.

"*Why*, might no' be as important as *who*," Caelen said. "If we knew *who* was behind this and *who* has Isobel and Aishlinn, we might be better able to help."

Nial let out an exasperated sigh. "I fear there are no answers here," he said as he ran a hand across his head. "I tell ye that I do no' enjoy the thought of tellin' me wife that I still dunnae why her da and brother did what they did or where her mum and sister be." The thought of returning to his wife without answers or without her family made him ill. A knot the size of a boulder had settled in his stomach.

"Then I say we quit this place and find the answers ye seek," Caelen told him. "And there be only one man I can think of at the moment, who has the answers." Caelen drank down the last of his ale, slammed the empty tankard onto the table and stood. A devious smile formed on his lips before he turned and sauntered out of the inn.

His friends looked up at him with raised eyebrows and perplexed expressions. They looked at one another and shrugged their broad shoulders. Following Caelen was better than sitting around an inn drinking and commiserating over the fact they had no answers.

TEN

Phillip Lindsay knew that most people did not like him. That fact did not bother him in the least. Truthfully, he had never been fond of most people. He preferred solitude to being surrounded by fawning feckless fools.

Fate had put him in what many would consider a most undesirable position. Phillip considered it a blessing. Born the second son of Carlich Lindsay, he had been left to his own devices most of his life. Second sons were of no real importance, for it was the first son who inherited everything. Therefore, all attention was paid to the first-born son, in this case, Seamus Lindsay.

Phillip hadn't been ignored so much as left alone. His mother -- mayhap in seeing how her husband fawned over Seamus, preparing him for his eventual succession as clan chief -- had tried to make up for her husband lack of interest in their younger son. And being kindred spirits, she spent more time with Phillip.

As a young boy, Phillip had possessed a vivid, creative imagination. He had learned early on however, that if he were to talk openly about the magical worlds he created, where men could fly and animals could speak, it not only earned him wary glances, but occasionally a swift smack to the back of his head. People thought him daft and fanciful, mayhap even a bit tetched.

His beautiful mum, however, had encouraged his creative pursuits, albeit with the caveat that such creative pursuits had to be done quietly and behind closed doors. It would not serve anyone well if people believed that Carlich Lindsay's son was tetched. Most people would not appreciate his vivid and colorful imagination.

He could remember his mother telling him that *"People do no' understand those who are different."*

Labeled *different* since the age of four, Phillip Lindsay had also learned to keep his thoughts and feelings hidden, deep down inside. His father taught him that boys and men do not cry, not even when someone they love dies. Even if that someone was your mother or your wife.

So when his dear mum passed away when he was eight years old, he did not cry. At least not openly, not in front of everyone. Nay, he stood bravely during her burial service, stoic and as quiet as a mouse in church, mimicking his father and his older brother.

But at the end of the day, he did cry. Hidden away in his room, his face buried in his pillow, he cried until he threw up.

As time went on, he withdrew even further into his own little world, where men flew, animals spoke, and little boys' beautiful mums never died. He stayed out of sight and out of the way, happily content with the solitude.

Over the years, Phillip had also learned to *listen*. Not just to the words that people spoke, but how they spoke them. He became very good at reading people's faces, their countenance, their little idiosyncrasies. Many times he would write down little things that he heard or witnessed so that he could refer to them later.

In an old trunk tucked away in a storage room, Phillip kept countless journals and scraps of parchments. He wrote fanciful tales and drew wild illustrations depicting what he saw in his mind's eye. He also kept very detailed logs of those who visited their keep.

Somehow, he took comfort in it, pretending that his mum wasn't really dead, but was instead travelling the world. Convinced he was that if and when she returned, she would want to know about all the things happened in her absence. As he grew older and time passed, he realized his mother was never coming back. But old habits die hard and he continued to keep detailed journals and records.

As he grew older, the label of *different* was gradually replaced with labels of *pompous* and *arrogant*. People simply did not understand him. He was far from pompous. He knew his own strengths and weaknesses. He knew he would never be the warrior that his brother, Seamus, had turned out to be. And he would never be the man his father so desperately wanted him to be.

After the three men had left him, Phillip paced around his study. He knew much more about the accusations against Angus than he led the men to believe. Phillip admired their steadfastness and their loyalty as it pertained to Angus McKenna. Not many people in this world deserved such fealty. It was a shame that the fool had thrown it all away.

Lost in his thoughts, he did not hear his lovely wife, Helena enter the room. He hadn't known she was there until he turned and nearly stumbled over her.

"God's teeth, woman!" he said with a start. "How many times have I told ye no' to sneak up on me like that?"

Helena's face lit up with a smile. Most people did not understand how someone as beautiful as Helena could love a man like Phillip Lindsay. She was a tiny, bonny thing, with hair the color of ginger and eyes as blue as the ocean. There were many times when Phillip asked himself what she saw in him.

The young beautiful woman loved him unconditionally and with ferocity that others might not be able to understand. Outward appearances were often deceiving. Helena too, had been labeled *different* at a very young age. She had been born with a slight deformity. Her left leg was a bit shorter than her right. It gave her an awkward gait and because of it she was constantly tormented by other children. The vicious taunting from uncaring fools continued, even when she grew older.

Her lot in life was made even more difficult by the fact that she had gone nearly fifteen years without uttering a single word. There had been no physical or medical reason for her muteness. Nay, it had been brought on by the traumatic way in which her parents had died when she was ten summers old. A man consumed with evil and malevolence had forced Helena and her father to watch as he raped her mum then slit her throat. Moments later, with the terrified Helena still watching, he killed her father.

Helena had never learned why the man had done what he had done or why he had allowed her to live. As she grew older, she supposed he had done it simply because he could. Until she met Phillip a few short years ago, she had lived her life in silence -- taunted and ridiculed by those who never took the time to understand her pain or her suffering.

Phillip Lindsay had fallen in love with her almost instantly.

Never known for acts of bravery or physical strength, somehow on that fateful day, Phillip found a part of him he did not know he owned.

Helena was being tormented by a group of young men. They had cornered her in an alley in Stirling. Mocking her, calling her names, they were doing their best to lift her skirts. Had Phillip not arrived Lord only knows what they would have done to her.

In an act of bravery, Phillip stepped in, with broadsword drawn, and fended off the three young men. One was left dead and another without his right arm, while the third had taken flight never to be seen or heard from again.

Perhaps Phillip had picked up a few things from all the years of watching his brother and father on the training fields. It was even possible that there was some latent talent for fighting that had remained dormant until it was needed. Whatever the cause of his sudden show of strength, he had been glad for it.

Phillip tucked an errant length of ginger hair behind his wife's ear with one hand while he caressed her swollen belly with the other. Helena stood on her tiptoes and gave him a peck on his cheek. "Are ye hungry, husband?" she asked him.

Cooking and baking was something his wife was very good at, as evidenced by all the weight he had gained since marrying her. He had always been on the thin side, until Helena came into his life. She had learned to cook and bake as a way of dealing with pain and heartache. Now, she had explained to him time and time again, she cooked and baked as a way of showing her love and gratitude for the man who saved her life.

"Wife, am I no' fat enough for ye now?" Phillip asked as he patted his large belly.

Helena looked him up and down with feigned scrutiny. "Aye, I suppose ye'll do."

Phillip rolled his eyes and drew her into a warm embrace. Her head barely reached his shoulders, a fact that he thoroughly enjoyed for he loved the way her hair smelled. Like lilacs and fresh bread.

Helena returned his hug and snuggled her head into his chest, turning slightly to the side for her stomach had grown so big over the past fortnight. "I ken ye be worried over Angus McKenna, husband. Is there naught I can do?"

There were many times over the past few years when Phillip was convinced his wife could read his mind. This was one of those moments. The events leading up to Angus' imprisonment weighed heavily on his conscience.

"Nay, lass, there is no' anything we can do now," he whispered into her hair. He did not like to keep secrets from his wife. But in this he would not yield to the temptation of sharing with her. The less she knew, the safer she and their babe would be.

The events of the past three years had led up to this moment in time. Phillip knew he was just as much a pawn in this game as Angus was. There were too many unknown players, unknown factors and that was a point he did not enjoy in the least. In just three days, if things played out as he worried they might, Angus McKenna would hang, alongside his son-in-law. Angus McKenna was a proverbial scapegoat in this melodrama.

Everything that I do, I do for Helena and my child, Phillip thought as he hugged his wife more tightly. Helena and their babe were his entire world. There was nothing he would not do to insure their safety and futures.

There was no room for feeling guilty. Angus was where he was because of the choices he had made. The only man Angus could blame was himself.

If Phillip Lindsay hoped to live long enough to see his first child born, there was not anything he could do to stop it.

ELEVEN

When Arline had told her husband about the MacDougalls at the gate and the three in his study, she could see his face light with an idea.

"Their timin' could no' be better," Carlich told her. "They can escort ye to Stirling."

Arline did not like the idea of going to Stirling and she most assuredly did not like the idea of complete strangers acting as escort. But, if the MacDougalls were as loyal and as fierce as Carlich had described them, then perhaps it might not be such a bad idea.

Carlich had asked very little of her over the past three years. Even if he was as old as dirt, he was still a kind man. He never yelled, never raised a hand to her and in short, had treated her with nothing but kindness and respect.

When she had come to Lindsay lands three years ago, she was a terrified lass of five and ten. Carlich had immediately put her at ease, letting her know the truth behind why her father had arranged their marriage and why Carlich had agreed to it.

Arline's father, Lord Orthanach Fitzgerald of Kildare, Ireland, had gotten himself into a good deal of trouble and owed some less-than-respectable men a good deal of money. Arline's mother, Frances, was one of Carlich's distant cousins. Frances had died when Arline was but ten. Without Frances there to keep Orthanach in check, he rapidly began a downward spiral, spending far more money than he had. By the time Arline was nearing her fifteenth birthday, Orthanach was so far in debt that he feared for his life. The men he owed the large sums to were not patient, nor were they the kind to wait until his financial situation improved.

Her father hadn't arranged the marriage as a means of protecting her, or for securing her future. It was simply a means to pay his debts, nothing more. After she and Carlich were married, Carlich had explained the situation to her fully. He had even admitted that he had been fully intending to reject Orthanach's offer of her hand. That was until he met her.

It wasn't so much her outward beauty that had attracted Carlich to her, but the spark of life evidenced in the way her green eyes twinkled with laughter over a ribald joke he had told her. She reminded him of his sister, long since dead and instinctively, Carlich wanted to protect her.

Carlich was a good, honest, even-tempered man, and for that, she loved him and cherished the friendship they had developed.

Scotland's future and its freedom potentially lay in her hands. With more than just the lives of Angus McKenna and Duncan McEwan hanging in the balance, she found it quite difficult to deny her husband his request.

Never in her life had she done anything even remotely dangerous. Before her mother's death, Arline had been raised to be a dutiful, quiet lady who would grow up to be a dutiful, quiet wife. Her destiny was to sit quietly, do as she was told, and never speak out of turn. Never put to voice any thoughts or feeling she might possess. Nay, good dutiful wives were genteel, quiet and unassuming. That was until she came to the Lindsay keep. Albeit she had yet to experience anything dangerous, she had been given more freedom than she had known before. Until now, the most dangerous thing she came in contact with was the bone needle she used for her embroidery.

With Carlich's help, Arline had found her voice and a backbone. He had always encouraged her to speak her mind, to believe in something bigger than herself and to hold tightly to her convictions. Aye, he was her husband, but he acted more like a grandfather spoiling a favorite grandchild than a husband.

Arline pondered the situation for a time. She worried about the safety of the keep in her absence. Aye, there would be plenty of people to care for Carlich. Knowing what she did now, she fretted over the safety of her people.

Her people. They were just as much hers as Seamus'. Seamus was gone more often than not. His wife had died a year before Arline had married Carlich. Arline was the lady of the keep, the chatelaine, and she did her best to make certain the keep ran smoothly. She loved these people, or at least most of them. She had no great fondness for Seamus or his arrogant son, Aric. Though she was used to their odd way of coming and going without leaving word, it still angered her that they had left with Carlich so close to death.

"Wife," Carlich sounded hopeful. "Will ye do this fer me?"

Arline gave his hand a gentle squeeze and smiled lovingly at him. "Aye, husband, I shall."

Suddenly, she felt quite energized by the thought of racing through the countryside, surrounded by a group of fierce Highlanders. The fact that her father would be appalled at such behavior made the idea even more enjoyable.

She looked away from her husband to ask the stranger a question only to find he was gone. He had managed to slip away without her notice.

Spies, Arline thought. Ye canna trust them.

"Yer a good woman, Arline," Carlich said as he patted her hand and closed his eyes. "A verra good woman."

Arline stood and kissed his forehead and straightened his blanket. "And ye are a good man, Carlich Lindsay," she whispered against his cold, clammy skin.

With her mind made up, she set off to see to the men who waited below stairs in her husband's study.

Daniel's felt his patience being sorely tested. He, along with Roy and Ronald, had been waiting for nearly an hour for Seamus Lindsay to come meet with them. Surely Seamus understood the importance of message he had been given earlier.

Roy and Ronald paced in opposite directions, mumbling curses under their breaths. They were just as offended as Daniel over being forced to wait for the Lindsay chief to grace them with his presence.

"Mayhap," Ronald began, "they did not relay the message accurately." He had paused before the fireplace and looked hopefully at his brother, Roy. "I be certain that the Lindsay would no' keep us waitin' like this if he knew the importance of the matter."

Roy was not as hopeful as Ronald. "I swear, if I find he's been tumblin' under the sheets with some kitchen maid while he makes us wait, I'll no' be responsible for me actions."

Ronald chuckled at his brother's threat. "I'll hold him down for ye, brother."

Daniel had been seated for more than a quarter hour, waiting for the door to open and the Lindsay chief to walk in. The longer he was made to wait the more his anger boiled. He had finally reached the end of his patience. Bolting to his feet, he headed toward the door, pausing to inform Roy and Ronald exactly what his intentions were.

"If the Lindsay will no' come to us, then *we* shall go to the Lindsay!" he seethed.

Roy and Ronald cast a glance at each other, shrugged their shoulders and nodded their heads in agreement. "I could no' agree with ye more, Daniel. We've waited long enough," Ronald said as they started toward the door.

Before they could reach the door, it opened with a rush of air, startling the three men. Their hopes at giving Seamus Lindsay a piece of their minds were quickly dashed.

With a swishing of silk skirts and the faint scent of lavender, a very comely young lass walked into the room. Auburn curls had been forced into a braid and looked as though they fought desperately for escape. She was taller than most women, with bright green eyes, and a very slender waist.

The three men stood silently for a moment while the lass scrutinized each of them in rapid succession. "Which of ye is Daniel?" she asked, forgoing formal introductions.

Daniel gave a slight bow at the waist. "I be Daniel," he answered with a tilt of his head and a smile.

She gave a curt nod and wasted no time getting to the heart of the matter. "I apologize for making ye wait, Daniel. Ye are here on behalf of Clan MacDougall." It was a statement, not a question. "How can I be of assistance?"

Daniel gave a furtive glance toward Roy and Ronald, who stood beside one another, looking just as perplexed as Daniel felt. Daniel noted a very distinct Irish accent and found it as intriguing as he did confusing. What was an Irish lass doing at the Lindsay keep and why was she here instead of Seamus?

"Pardon me, lass, but we are here to speak with Seamus," he told her. He began to think that Ronald was correct in his assumption that the message had not been delivered correctly.

The lass folded her hands in front of her, her expression unchanged. "I ken that. But Seamus is no' available at the moment. I act in his stead."

Three sets of brows knotted in simultaneous confusion. "I beg yer pardon lass, but we must speak with Seamus. Please, deliver to him the message that we come to --"

She held her hand up to stop him. "I ken verra well *why* ye are here. Ye invoke the bond of the seven. I am fully aware of that bond, Daniel. Again, I tell ye that I act in Seamus' stead."

Daniel was growing quite frustrated, but managed to hold his temper in. He had no idea who the redheaded young lass was nor did he know why Seamus was refusing to meet with them. The lack of soldiers at the border and the lack of men within the castle made the hair on his neck stand up.

"Are ye his daughter?" Roy asked, his ire plainly evident.

She took a slight pause before answering. "Nay, I am no' his daughter."

The three men cast more curious glances at one another as their confusion and frustration grew. Daniel decided it was time to take control of the situation. "Lass, pardon our confusion. But *who* are ye and *why* are ye acting in Seamus' stead?"

With a lift of her chin she pulled her shoulders back and looked Daniel in the eye. "I am Lady Arline Lindsay, wife of Carlich Lindsay. Seamus is no' here."

The three men could not hide their astonishment. Their eyes snapped open along with their jaws.

Lady Arline had grown accustomed to the reactions she received when she announced who her husband was. While she may have been accustomed to the astonished looks and the way people whispered behind her back, it did not mean she was unbothered by them.

With a slight shake of her head and a roll of her eyes, she placed her hands on her hips. "Lads, close your mouths. Ye be no bairns, ye're men full grown. Arranged marriages should not be such a shock to ye."

Daniel was instantly embarrassed by her direct chastisement. He could feel his face burn. Roy and Ronald cleared their throats, but remained quiet. Daniel attempted to apologize for being rude. "I do apologize, my lady," he said. "It is just that --"

Again she stopped him with a wave of her hand. "Aye, aye," she began. "I be *much* younger than my husband. It canna be the first time you've ever heard of an older man marryin' a younger woman," her tone was firm and direct. "Now, let us get back to why ye be here and what ye need of us."

Daniel was uncertain if her blunt, to-the-point attitude was a simple matter of who she was or if she was in a hurry to hear them out before sending them on their way. His jaw clenched with annoyance.

Two could play at this game. "Since ye state that yer fully aware of the bond of the seven, then ye already ken what we need."

"Ye canna have it," was her curt response. "So ye best be on your way." She gave a quick nod of her head and started to turn around to leave.

"What do ye mean *we canna have it?*" Daniel asked angrily. "If ye be fully informed of the bond, then ye ken ye canna deny us."

Lady Arline let loose an irritated sigh. "Daniel," she began. "I canna give what I do no' have."

He wasn't sure how much more of this talking in circles he could withstand. Mayhap the young woman didn't understand as much as she would like them to believe. He took a steady breath before speaking. "M'lady, are ye aware that Angus McKenna and his son-in-law are now sittin' in prison in Edinburgh and that they have been sentenced to hang?"

He saw it then, just a flash of surprise in her green eyes. It was gone as quickly as it had appeared. His instincts were correct. She *didn't* know as much as she was letting on.

"Hanged?" she whispered softly before she waded through the wall of men and began to pace. "But he's not supposed to hang," she murmured, still pacing with her eyes cast to the floor, her arms crossed below her bosom. "Nay, that wasna supposed to happen," she murmured.

The three men watched as she paced, growing more confused with each statement she uttered. Daniel began to reassess his previous belief that she didn't know anything.

"Lass, what do ye mean this was no' supposed to happen?" Roy asked, unable to keep his curiosity in check any longer.

Lady Arline gave a quick shake of her head and waved away his question as if he were a pesky bee buzzing around her head. "Allow me to think, please," she told him gruffly.

The men looked at one another again. This lass was as confusing a creature as any they'd ever encountered. Daniel was trying to be as patient as he could while the lass paced and mumbled. He couldn't help to continue wonder where Seamus was.

After several long moments of pacing and mumbling, Daniel could take no more. "M'lady, we have no' much time. Angus and Duncan will be taken to Stirling soon, to hang. And their wives are missin', along with Duncan's babes. 'Tis verra important that ye tell us *why* they weren't supposed to hang."

Arline stopped pacing and looked at him as if he were some peculiar object. "Their wives are not missing and neither are their babes."

That was news to Daniel and his men. No one had seen Isobel, Aishlinn or the babes since the night the bastards came for Angus and Duncan. As far as any of the three men were aware, no one knew if the women had left voluntarily or if they'd been taken.

"Ye mean ye ken where they be?" Ronald asked, bewilderedly.

She refused to answer the question and instead, let out a long, heavy sigh as she studied the three men closely. "I think I should take ye to Carlich now," she said as she headed toward the door.

Daniel, Roy, and Ronald were riddled with confusion. Daniel began to wish that he had stayed behind and sent David in his stead. With a shrug of their shoulders, they followed the lovely redheaded lass out of the room.

Daniel, Roy, and Ronald stood at Carlich Lindsay's bedside. So stunned were they with the information the auld man had just shared with them that the slightest breeze would have knocked them over.

"Ye canna be serious, Carlich." Daniel exclaimed breathlessly.

"Aye, I am, lad. I need ye to guard me young wife with yer lives. See her safely to Stirling. Scotland, lads, is depending on ye." It was growing more difficult for Carlich to speak without losing his breath or bringing on a violent coughing spasm.

Arline sat beside him with a wet cloth. Carlich could not die in peace until he knew that he had done everything he could to see that the wrong was righted.

Arline bent forward and whispered in her husband's ear. He responded with an affirmative nod. Without turning away from her husband she spoke over her shoulder to Daniel. "We shall let my husband rest now."

The MacDougall men remained quiet while Arline wiped her husband's brow and gave his arm a gentle pat. "I shall return shortly, husband. I shall leave you to Meg, but I ask that ye rest."

For the first time in many weeks, Carlich did not argue with her request. He simply returned her smile and nodded his head slightly before closing his eyes.

From his vantage point Daniel could tell that Arline held a strong affection for her husband. He wondered briefly at how many women of her age would stay with a man of Carlich's age, or sit beside his deathbed.

Arline kissed her husband's forehead again. She left instructions with Meg, one of the servants, before leading the men out of the room.

"I've never in my life done anything such as what Carlich is askin' of me." Arline told the men as she led them down the hallway. "I can only promise ye that I will do my best to be as little trouble to ye as possible."

Neither Daniel, Roy nor Ronald liked the idea of escorting the fine young lady to Stirling. It was far too dangerous for such a young lady. Were it anyone but Angus and Duncan's necks that were at risk, they would have argued more forcefully against the idea. But circumstances being what they were, they knew they had very little choice in the matter.

Ronald had argued that mayhap Arline should stay behind and allow them to carry the information and the documents to Stirling. But Carlich argued against it. His reasons, when one thought them out, made sense. If men from the MacDougall Clan showed up with the documents, it could be argued that the documents were forged and held nothing more than lies created by men who wanted to help their chief.

It had to be Lady Arline who presented the documents to Robert Stewart.

TWELVE

The wagon taking Angus and Duncan to Stirling was dark and reeked of sweat, urine and fear, no doubt left behind by its prior occupants. The breeze flittering in through the bars did nothing more than swirl the stench. Angus felt that no amount of soap and water would ever get rid of the foul smell. The only solution to getting rid of it would be to set the wagon afire.

Rain fell steadily against the roof of the wagon. It reminded Angus of ham frying in a skillet, which in turn made his stomach growl and his mouth water. With his eyes closed, he leaned against the wall of the wagon and thought of home.

What he would not give to be back there, home, to smell baking bread wafting through the air, or better yet, some of Mary's sweet cakes. He missed everything about Castle Gregor, from the stables to the pastures to Mary's kitchen to his private chambers and everything in between.

He could picture the rolling hills and the way the tall grass waved in the breeze. The sound of the wind as it danced through the treetops would seem like music to his ears right now. He could hear the blacksmith banging his hammer against the anvil, sheep bleating from the hill and the newborn calves crying to be fed.

He pictured the children running from the courtyard to the top of the hill, their laughter floating along the summer breeze, none of them with a care in the world. There were many times, such as now, when he wished he could go back in time and be a child again. He sometimes wondered what he would change and what he would want to remain the same.

A tremendous sense of melancholy began to settle into his bones as they travelled to Stirling. Angus longed to be *home,* where he would plunge himself into the loch and take his grandsons fishing.

Between his blood children and those he adopted, he now had fourteen grandchildren: eleven boys and three girls. He would miss watching them grow up.

More than anything else, however, Angus missed his wife. Isobel was as good a woman as could be found. She was beautiful, strong and intelligent. What he would not give to run his fingers through her raven-black hair and breathe in the scent of her, to wrap his arms around her and hold her for eternity.

He knew he didn't deserve her. She loved him fiercely and without reserve. He owed her his life, for it was Isobel who had gotten him through the most difficult heartache any man could endure: the loss of the woman he loved and the child she carried. Angus had fallen into a deep depression when he had learned of Laiden's death. He took to drinking every waking hour of the day. Had Isobel not been there to help him climb out of the abyss, he most assuredly would not be alive today.

He hadn't known at the time however, that 'twas all a lie, that the woman he loved and their babe in fact lived. It had been his own brother who had betrayed him, lied to him in order that he could have Laiden for himself.

There were times when he did wonder how differently his life would have been had he not believed his brother. Had he gone in search of her and found Laiden, he would not now be married to Isobel and they would never have had Bree.

It amazed him how one small lie, one small act, could affect the lives of countless people. Such as the lie he was now embroiled in. Lies, deceit, and greed -- things he could not abide and had never engaged in until the past few years. Had he known then what he knew now, he might have chosen a different path.

But as it was, it was too late to change things. He had made his bed and now, he must hang in it.

THIRTEEN

While four outriders led the way down a narrow road that snaked around a very large hill, the wagon driver hugged the road to his left. At times, the wheels brushed against the jagged rocks of the hill. He decided it was better to battle against those rocks, than take the risk of falling off the cliff.

The rain had turned to a light mist some time ago, giving hope that the sun might someday shine again. It would take a fortnight of continuous sunlight to dry out the mud. The horses trudged through thick mud and deeply rutted roads making the journey north all the more perilous and difficult. The driver urged his team of four horses on with threats of turning them into stew if they did not get him safely down the road.

They were rounding another bend when one of the outriders called out for them to halt. The wagon driver brought his team to an abrupt halt, which jostled his passengers awake.

Something lay ahead, in the middle of the road, and blocked their passage. From where he sat, he could not see clearly what it was, only that the four outriders had surrounded it. Years of experience warned him something was amiss. He scanned the woods to his right, looking for any sign of trouble. Nothing appeared out of the ordinary, but he knew that did not necessarily mean all was well.

It took a few moments for him to realize that it was a child who sat huddled in the middle of the road. The driver could barely make out the child's wailing as he watched the outriders quickly dismount.

"What goes on here?" one of the outriders asked the boy.

Between sobs, the lad cried out his answer. "Our wagon fell off the road!" he wailed as he pointed to the embankment. The remaining guards came to see what had caused the caravan to stop. "Me mum and da and baby sister are trapped!" the lad cried out. His dirty face was streaked with tears and his shoulders continued to shake.

The men quickly dismounted and without question, started to make their way down the steep drop off to help the injured. It was, mayhap, *not* the wisest decision they could have made.

It had been three long years since their last good adventure. Maggy's boys had grown much in that time. Besides gaining height, weight, and muscles, they had been fortunate enough to train with some of the best Highland warriors in all of Scotland.

Robert, the oldest, was nearly seven and ten now and taller than his adoptive father, Findley, by two inches. His younger brother Andrew was not nearly as tall, but at four and ten, he was developing muscle and speed. Collin was the same age as Andrew. But where Andrew was stocky, Collin was tall and lean.

The twins, Liam and Ian, were growing up to be strapping young lads. Much to their mother's dismay -- but to their adoptive father's pride -- both had been blessed with a remarkable, natural skill with the sword. 'Twas a talent the lads of almost ten and one took great pleasure in displaying to anyone who would watch. While their mum would have preferred they took up less dangerous pursuits, she could not deny their talent.

The five boys were quite thankful that the Good Lord had blessed their mum with two daughters to fawn over. With Maggy's attention focused on their sweet sisters, Deidre and Elizabeth, the boys were able to avoid their mum's ever-watchful eye and overprotective nature.

Therefore it had taken Robert completely by surprise when his mum came to him yesterday, with a plan that involved not only Robert and his brothers, but also several women and other children of their clan. Mayhap were he older and wiser he would have attempted to talk his mother out of the ludicrous idea. But he was itching for adventure and quite anxious to put to use the skills he had learned these past few years.

He had to admit that his mother's plan was not *completely* ridiculous. And it was for a good cause he reckoned. If his father hadn't instilled in the boys the importance of honor, of always doing the right thing -- even when no one was watching -- and to always help those who were less fortunate, they wouldn't be here right now. Robert supposed his father would have no one to blame but himself. Besides, he was only doing what his mother told him to do -- again, as his father had taught him.

No matter how he tried to justify his actions this day, he knew deep down his father was going to be angry. And if they somehow managed to succeed with his mother's plan he also knew Findley would not be able to deny that he was, in fact, quite proud.

Though Findley never raised a hand to the boys, there were far worse methods of punishment. Robert shuddered when he thought of how many months of cleaning latrines lay in his future. It would be worth it, he believed, if not for honor then for the chance to put his skills to good use

They had stayed up half the night going over the plan, again and again. Robert had it burned into his memory. He was glad that Findley had taught them how to think on their feet. For a brief moment as they waited beside the road, he wished his father was here to offer assistance. But he knew that if Findley had caught wind of their plan, they would not be here at this moment. Instead, he and his brothers would be back at home trying to keep Deirdre out of trouble.

Crouched low, hiding in the bushes, Robert wiped his sweaty palms on his shirt and unsheathed his sword. His brothers were well hidden just a few paces away. He could just make out Collin's form and he knew Andrew was not far from Collin.

Please, God, let everything go accordin' to plan, Robert thought quietly. And please, if ye could, let da no' be too angry with what we are about to do.

Angus and Duncan had no way of knowing what was happening. Apparently, whatever was happening was happening ahead of them. Puzzled, they looked at one another, shrugged their shoulders and went to the side of the wagon to get a better look. They were too far away from the commotion to see anything, but they could hear. Someone was shouting, but it was too muffled to make out what was being said. A moment later, the guards who had been following behind them kicked their horses and headed past the wagon and toward the ruckus.

"What do ye suppose is happenin'?" Duncan asked.

Angus' brow creased as he shook his head. "I dunnae," he answered. "But I think those guards will be in a heap of trouble if anyone learns they left their posts."

As they sat next to one another, straining their ears to listen, another commotion broke out. Suddenly, the wagon was being rocked back and forth, jostling the two men into one another. More shouting commenced as the wagon continued to rock back and forth.

"Do ye hear that, Angus?" Duncan asked.

"Aye, I hear it," he answered in disbelief. Some of the shouts sounded quite feminine while others sounded like they belonged to children. "What the bloody hell?" he whispered under his breath.

Finally, the wagon stopped its rocking and the air around them became quiet. They still could not see what had happened and the mounted guards had yet to return. Time passed in relative confusion. Angus and Duncan continued to listen.

Then the wagon suddenly bolted forward, throwing Angus and Duncan into the gate. As the horses pulled them along, they passed by a most befuddling site. Lining the side of the road were the mounted guards, as naked as the day they were born, with hands and feet bound and pieces of cloth either tied around their mouths or stuffed into them.

Five women of varying ages stood behind them, with broadswords drawn, some with bows and arrows strapped to their backs, and wry smiles on their faces. The women waved -- one wiggled her fingers and winked -- looking proud as peahens as the wagon drove by. Neither Angus nor Duncan recognized any of the women.

"What the blazes?" Duncan muttered as he absentmindedly waved back at the women. "I be no' sure, Angus, but I think we're bein' kidnapped."

Not long after, three young lads and three women all on horseback fell in behind the wagon. Angus' heart fell to his stomach. "Nay, no' kidnapped," he said with a shake of his head. "But someone does no' want us to make it to Stirling."

It hadn't taken long or a huge leap in deduction for him to figure out who was behind their capture. In no time, they were going at breakneck speed around the bend and down the hill. With each twist and turn, Angus and Duncan were thrown into one another, jostled about like onions in a bowl.

They travelled for quite a distance before the madman driving the wagon, thankfully, slowed down to a less terrifying speed. The wagon veered left and soon they were crashing through thick, dense shrubbery, bushes, and brush. The wagon tipped and rocked, and once again, Angus and Duncan were thrown into each other.

He could take no more of it. Mustering all his strength, Angus rose to his knees and began pounding on the wall behind the driver.

"Bree McKenna!" he shouted as he pounded on the wall. Duncan was lying flat on his back, staring up at Angus. It took a few moments for awareness to settle in.

"Nay!" he shouted at Angus. "Ye do no' believe," his words were cut short when the wagon jerked hard to the left and Angus fell sideways on top of him. Duncan grunted and cursed as they scrambled to right themselves.

Angus took a deep breath and let loose with a litany of curses before drawing himself back up to his knees. Duncan joined him in the assault on the heavy wooden wall.

"Bree! I swear when I get me hands on ye!" Duncan bellowed.

"I do no' care if ye be married and a mum, I swear I will show ye no mercy!" Angus yelled loudly. *How on earth could me daughter be so daft!* He wondered between shouting threats and pounding his fists on the wall.

Their threats fell on deaf ears. After some time, Angus gave up and slid down the wall to sit. If it was his daughter Bree driving the wagon, Angus knew she would not stop until they had reached their destination or when she was good and ready. He blamed Bree's stubbornness on her mother.

Duncan finally gave up and sat down next to Angus. Frustrated, he thrust his legs out, crossed them at the ankles as he crossed his arms over his chest. "Does she no' understand the trouble she will be in?"

Angus grunted and shook his head. "Nay, I do no' believe she does." He knew as well that she did not understand the importance of him and Duncan getting to Stirling.

Had they made it to Stirling in time, there was a good chance they could have avoided the hanging. But now? Who knew what Robert Stewart would think of Angus and Duncan's obvious escape? Bree could not know it at the moment, but she may as well have put the nooses around their necks with her own hands.

FOURTEEN

"I'm going to kill her," Nial ground out. "I'm going to kill her!" The vein in his forehead pulsed with each furious beat of his heart. His face was red with anger that bordered on unadulterated rage.

Caelen grabbed the halter of Nial's horse and stopped him from doing just that. "Wait!" Caelen whispered hoarsely.

Nial shot him an exasperated look. "Let go of me horse, Caelen McDunnah. I've no wish to kill a friend this day."

A roguish grin formed on Caelen's lips. "Funny, I was just thinkin' the same thing."

Nial's jaw clenched as he glared furiously at Caelen and wondered what his friend could possibly be thinking by trying to stop him.

Rowan and Findley stood between the men and watched. Rowan found himself thanking the Good Lord for giving him a quiet wife who never gave him a moment's trouble. Worry, yes, but the kind of trouble Bree gave Nial? Never.

Findley was just as angry as Nial at what he had just witnessed. Inwardly, he felt more than a swell of pride at how well his sons had handled themselves against the guards, though he'd never admit as much to any of them.

He also knew that more likely than not, his hardheaded wife had planned the entire thing. He supposed the only reason he hadn't seen her was that she had stayed back at their keep to take care of their daughters. Her absence also afforded her some plausible deniability.

But Findley knew the entire attack had his wife's name written all over it. As soon as he returned home, he was going to have a very long talk with his beautiful wife. It was in her favor that it would be days before he could do just that. Mayhap by the time he saw her next, he wouldn't be angry enough to turn her over his knee.

"Listen to me, Nial," Caelen said firmly.

"I'll listen to ye *after* I stop my foolish wife."

After they had gotten nowhere with Phillip Lindsay or with anyone else in Edinburgh, they had decided to go to Stirling. They also decided that mayhap twenty-five mounted guards might not be enough to protect Angus and Duncan.

It was certainly plausible that whoever had put Angus and Duncan in jail might want to ensure that they did in fact die, either by hanging or by attacking the caravan on its way to Stirling. Dead men could not speak, nor could they point accusing fingers.

If Caelen's gut was correct, there were reasons why Angus had admitted guilt and they had nothing to do with the man actually being guilty. So they set out to follow the wagon, keeping at a safe distance. They stayed far enough away so as not to be seen yet close enough that they could react to any potential attack.

The thought that anyone would attack to *free* the two men had never entered any of their minds.

"This may work in Angus' favor, Nial," Caelen explained. "If we can keep their necks out of the hangman's noose, it might give us time to find out the truth behind all of this. It might also give us time to find Isobel and Aishlinn."

The bulging vein in Nial's head continued to throb rapidly while he weighed Caelen's argument.

"Ye can paddle yer wife's bottom *after* we find out the truth," Caelen offered with a grin.

Nial took in a deep breath and let it out very slowly. He knew all to well how stubborn his wife could be. He also knew how smart she was.

But this? Attacking royal guards? Leaving them stripped naked along the road? Stealing the wagon and driving it off like the devil was chasing them? Nay, this was beyond anything he could ever have imagined her doing.

Lady Arline Lindsay had done exceedingly well at keeping her word *not* to be a bother to the MacDougall men. In turn, they had shown her nothing but kindness, offering her words of encouragement as they raced along the country toward Stirling. A few had even gone so far as to offer to let her sleep atop their laps. Graciously, she had refused them.

She did not want to take her newfound courage *too* far. She was, after all, a lady in all respects and she had husband waiting for her at home. And considering the circumstances they were travelling under, she did not want to sully the reputation of Clan Lindsay.

"Are ye sure ye do no' need to rest, my lady?" Ronald asked as they made their way across a wide valley.

Arline smiled politely as she answered. "Nay, Ronald, but I do thank ye kindly."

It was difficult to embrace the reality that she was on her way to Stirling. No matter how tired, wet, sore or hungry she became, she refused to give in to the temptation of resting. Too many people, too many lives depended on her making it to Stirling. Time was of the essence.

It was unsettling to think that only the day before, she thought of herself as nothing more than her husband's caregiver. Nothing lay in her future other than waiting for Carlich to die. It wasn't as if she wished he would hurry up and be done with it. On the contrary, the longer her husband lived the more time she spent away from her father.

Her father was not particularly mean to her. He'd rarely ever raised a hand to her in anger, save for when she was a small child. He saw that she was properly educated and had the proper clothes as well as a roof over her head. For that, she would always be grateful to him for she knew her life could have been drastically different. She could have ended up living in abject poverty like her half-sisters. Arline knew that were it not for her sneaking them every spare coin that she could, Morralyn and Geraldine would have ended up as bar wenches or worse yet, working in some squalid brothel somewhere in Inverness.

Orthanach had never publicly -- nor privately for that matter -- recognized the daughters who were born to two different women and on the wrong side of the blanket. Shamefully, he had used women without any thought as to what might happen should any of them bear him a child and then tossed them aside unceremoniously with no remorse or guilt. Arline knew exactly what he thought of the women he bedded for he had told her on more than one occasion. They were *less* simply because they'd been born that way.

Oh! How she wished Morralyn and Geraldine were here now! She resisted the urge to giggle at that thought. Morralyn would have been batting her eyelashes at every eligible man present. While Morralyn flirted, Geraldine would have observed quietly, hiding her smile behind her hands. And knowing the two of them as she did, they would have found trouble, or trouble would have found them.

The sound of Daniel's voice broke her train of thought. Or was it David? The brothers looked so much alike that it was difficult to tell one from the other unless she was close enough to see their eyes. Daniel's were blue, David's green. "It will no' be long now, my lady. We should reach Stirling before dawn."

Dawn? How would one be able to tell dawn from dusk with the dark gray sky and rain? Quietly she wondered if she would not succumb to exhaustion and fall from her horse before the night was through. Not wanting to sound spoiled or ungrateful for their service, she remained mute and kept the thought to herself.

Arline glanced at the man riding next to her and saw his green eyes. "Thank you, David," she said.

David gave her a thoughtful smile. "'Tis more than a good deed yer doin' fer us, m'lady," he said as his smile slowly faded away.

Arline had no response. She was not doing this to gain anyone's favor or praise. This was the only right decision she could have made. Had she denied her husband's request and lives were lost, there would have been no way she could have lived with herself. Guilt would have followed her all the rest of her days. Nay, this was the *right* thing to do.

Phillip Lindsay rarely, if ever, yelled. But yell he did when he learned that Angus and Duncan had escaped. If it had not been for his wife's soothing voice and the pained expression on her face, he might very well have torn his study to shreds.

It had to be the MacDougalls who had perfected the escape. Phillip doubted anyone else had the ballocks to do such a thing. While he very well may have admired the fealty and loyalty the MacDougall clan felt toward their chief, he could not let them go unpunished.

In hindsight, he should have sent more than twenty-five guards to take the fools to Stirling. Shaking his head in dismay, Phillip realized he could have sent one thousand men and it would not have mattered. The MacDougall warriors would have found a way to rescue their chief. They were relentless bastards.

"Damn them all," Phillip seethed as he paced around his office. His under-sheriff stood fearfully in front of Phillip's desk. He dared not speak.

"And our men have turned up *nothing?*" Phillip asked incredulously.

"Nay," the under-sheriff answered with a slight tremor to his voice.

The guards had sat naked beside the road for hours before they were discovered. A dispatch had been sent to Stirling as well as to Edinburgh. Nearly a full day had passed by the time he had received the news.

"We've only just received this news. I've sent as many men as I could, some seventy men, sir, to search for them."

Seventy or seven thousand, Phillip's gut told him it would not matter. Knowing the MacDougalls as he did, they were long gone and had Angus and Duncan safely hidden. He wondered how Angus could have orchestrated the escape from his prison cell. Could one of the guards have been bribed to help affect the escape?

Angus was loved by more people than just his clansmen. There were many people who admired and respected the man. Phillip had no doubt that there were far more people who would not, could not believe the news that Angus was a confessed traitor. Few, if any, would turn away from the man, admitted traitor or not. How many would offer the men refuge? How many would open their doors to the two men?

The better question was how many would be willing to risk their own lives, or the lives of their families, for Angus'?

Though he did not like where his train of thought took him, Phillip was left with no other options. He stopped pacing and turned to his under-sheriff.

"Issue warrants for the MacDougall warriors," he began as he went to his desk and began taking out his writing implements. "Spread word that anyone, and I do mean *anyone* who is found harboring Angus McKenna or Duncan McEwan will be hanged, along with their wives and their children."

The under-sheriff stood with mouth agape and eyes wide. "But," he began to speak. Phillip held him off with a wave of his hand.

"They are admitted traitors. Anyone who harbors them will be considered traitors to king and country, an act punishable by hanging. I'll no' argue this with ye. Mayhap people will no' be so willing to help Angus and Duncan if they worry they'll hang alongside them."

Phillip could only hope he would not have to make good on his threat. He had no desire to hang anyone. He continued to scratch out warrants and missives while his under-sheriff stood solemnly and waited.

As soon as he was finished, he affixed his seal with red wax and handed the documents over. "Make sure word spreads quickly," he told him. "And make certain no one doubts me word."

The under-sheriff took the documents, gave a quick bow at his waist and quit the room. As soon as the man left, Phillip's wife appeared before him.

"Certainly ye do no' truly intend to hang women and children?" she asked as she stood in the doorway to his office.

He saw an expression on his wife's face that he had never seen before. Shame.

Helena was his world. She and their babe were the only reason he climbed out of bed each morning. Without her, he was nothing but a body taking up space. She did not understand why he was doing what he was doing. He had kept his secrets hidden from her for a very long time. Not because he did not think her capable of understanding or because he worried she'd not be able to keep the secrets closely guarded. It was for her safety, and now, their babe's that he held on to his secrets.

Guilt tugged at his heart. He could not live without her. He would not be able to live with himself if anything happened to her or their child. Phillip also knew that things would never be the same between them if he made good on his promise to hang anyone who offered aid to Angus and Duncan. He would never be able to look at her again if he knew she was ashamed of him.

Nay, he could not live with causing her any pain, nor could he abide it if she thought him a disgrace. This day was growing worse as the moments ticked by. Keep his wife in complete ignorance in order to keep her safe and risk earning her life-long disrespect and let her think him a disgrace. Or, tell her the truth and risk her death. Neither option was at all pleasing.

Despite his concerns, he decided it was time perhaps, to tell her the truth.

"Wife," he said soberly. "We need to talk."

FIFTEEN

Wee William and his men had been waiting for the perfect time to enter Castle Stirling. It hadn't been easy for any of them to stand by and do nothing. There wasn't a man among them who did not wish to take a battering ram to the front door, rush in like a swarm of bees, find Robert Stewart and demand that he listen.

But Wee William knew acting in such a manner would not help their cause.

Instead of invading the castle, Wee William and his men camped on the outskirts of Stirling. It wasn't as if they were trying to remain hidden. Nay, once word had spread that Angus and Duncan were being brought to Stirling, the town's population seemed to triple in a matter of a few short days.

As was typical with the hangings of important persons, people had come from miles around. Usually the town or city would take on a fair-like atmosphere, filling near to bursting with jugglers, troubadours, musicians and acrobats along with those wishing to observe the hangings with their own eyes. Wee William assumed many of the people milling about the town wanted to say they were there the day they hanged the traitors Angus McKenna and Duncan McEwan.

This was not a story he looked forward to someday telling his grandchildren.

What would become of their clan, should Angus and Duncan hang? He could not afford to think on that prospect now. He had to concentrate on doing whatever he could to ensure the hangings did not take place.

Even if that meant sneaking into the castle and finding Robert Stewart.

And if that didn't work, he was not above breaking the two men out before they hanged and getting them out of the country. He chuckled softly at that thought and wondered what his dear wife would say to living in France.

"Wee William! Wee William!" Black Richard came tearing through the clearing on horseback. From the expression on his face and the sound of his voice, Wee William felt certain he was not going to like the news Black Richard was bringing.

Wee William stood up from the fallen tree he'd been using as a seat and hurried to Black Richard. "What is it?" he demanded as Black Richard slid from his horse, out of breath and covered in sweat. Or rain. It was difficult to ascertain at the moment for it hadn't stopped raining in days.

"'Tis Angus and Duncan!" Black Richard said as he stopped to catch his breath. "They've been taken!"

Wee William's brow wrinkled with confusion. "What do ye mean *taken*?"

Black Richard bent and rested his palms on his knees. Between gulps, he answered. "Someone took them yesterday. A band of brigands, the guards say. At least one hundred men they say. Over-powered the guards and left them naked along the road. They took the wagon and no one knows where they be."

Wee William chewed on that information for a time. Why not kill the guards? Why would they leave them naked beside the road? Who would have taken Angus and Duncan and for what purpose? Did they mean to ensure they died?

A hundred questions banged about in his mind as he paced the forest floor. If the people who took Angus and Duncan were not friends or allies, then their lives were in grave danger. Perhaps whoever took them were the real traitors and worried over being found out. Killing Angus and Duncan would ensure their secret was safe and they could continue on with their treacherous deeds. That thought made his stomach tighten with dread and anger.

If, however, the individuals responsible for taking them were in fact friends, it still did not bode well for the two men. An escape such as this would make them appear all the more the traitors they were accused of being.

A number of unpleasant scenarios played out in his mind. All of them ended with the deaths of his chief and the man he considered the closest thing to a brother that he had.

Black Richard had managed to get his breathing under control and stood patiently waiting for instructions from Wee William. Several of the other men had heard the news and they stood near Black Richard and watched as their leader paced and shook his head. They were just as bewildered and baffled as Wee William, but stood quietly, allowing him to process the information.

Finally, the giant stopped pacing and turned to look at his men.

"We need to find Angus and Duncan. We know not *who* took them, but friend or foe, we need to find them before Phillip Lindsay's men do."

Black Richard nodded in agreement. But a question lingered. "What do we do when we find them, Wee William?"

Wee William shook his head and headed toward the horses. He pulled his saddle from the ground and tossed it on the bay gelding's back.

"I have no' idea, Black Richard."

If foes had taken the two men, then Wee William could argue that fact in front of Robert Stewart, if he ever found the fool. That fact could only work in his chief's favor.

However, if friends had taken Angus and Duncan, he knew an altogether different scenario would play out. Aye, he would at the very least be able to breathe more easily knowing they still lived.

At the moment, Wee William was not certain who he hoped had taken Angus and Duncan. No matter who had taken them, the outcome would undoubtedly be the same. Angus and Duncan would hang at dawn.

SIXTEEN

Fury erupted behind his eyes as the maid lay at his feet. The anger roared quietly, like the flames in a blacksmith's forge. Hot enough to melt iron -- or to kill.

Years of experience had taught him how to kill silently, mercilessly, and without any evidence left behind to point in his direction. He chuckled inwardly. No one would ever think he could do such a thing. People loved him. Adored him. Admired him. Well, *almost* everyone.

The maid's death had been unfortunate, but necessary. She had known far too much. She wasn't even *aware* that she knew anything and she wasn't bright enough to put the pieces together. But should anyone ask the right questions too soon....

He couldn't take the chance. Not yet, not when he was so close to the end goal. Very soon he would have all that he ever wanted.

Shaking his head, he looked down at the dead girl and quietly sighed. It *was* quite unfortunate for she had been such a pretty little thing. He shrugged it off as another sacrifice of war. And this *was* war.

He put out the candle with his fingertips and quietly left the larder. It would be hours before anyone found her body and he'd be long gone by then. Without question, the little maid had told him everything that she knew. Her lady was on her way to Stirling, guarded by a band of MacDougall men. When he pressed her further, the maid had admitted to overhearing parts of the conversation. *"The lady has a box that the laird gave her. I dunnae what be in the box, but they say it has somethin' to do with Angus McKenna. Somethin' that can stop him from hangin'."*

Damn Carlich Lindsay. He would have loved to strangle the auld man too, but one dead person was enough. The maid's death was going to cause a big enough uproar as it was. Two dead people could very well have brought everything tumbling down. He was too close, far too close to begin making mistakes now.

Meticulously he had planned for every eventuality, or so he thought. Damn Arline Lindsay. *Her* he would enjoy killing. But he could not be in two places at once. As he made his way quietly out of the keep and into the dark night, he quickly formed a new plan. He hadn't gotten where he was by letting small distractions get in his way. He hadn't let anyone get in his way.

He was at least a day's ride behind Arline and the MacDougalls.

Hopefully the fools were taking their time in getting to Stirling. He must hurry if he were to keep her from getting there before Angus was hanged.

In no time he had made his way out of the keep and beyond its walls, making no more noise than a mouse. He had to make certain that Lady Arline Lindsay did not make it to Stirling, at least not alive. And he had to get that damned box away from her.

Who knew what information it held. He cursed under his breath for underestimating Carlich. The man was as auld as dirt for the sake of Christ! What could he possibly know? What information could he have gained laying on his deathbed all these years?

Nay, he couldn't know anything. 'Twas impossible. Mayhap the auld man had lost his mind and the box held nothing of import. Mayhap it was the auld man's attempt at one last good deed before death took him. How could he possibly know anything when he hadn't left his damned room in the past year?

The soft rain helped cover any sound he might have made and washed away any trail he might have left behind. He made his way across the grass and into the woods where his men were waiting for him. He pushed away the uneasiness and convinced himself that there was no possible way that Carlich knew anything. The box was probably empty, or, at the most, it simply held a letter that spoke of all the good Angus McKenna had done for the people of Scotland.

Bah! Angus was just as guilty as he was. He had plotted right alongside him. But plans had been put in place on the off chance the fool had a change of heart or tried to save his own neck. He knew there was naught Angus would not do for his wife and children. Isobel and Aishlinn were ensconced, along with those brats of Duncan's, in a safe place. He had been very careful with them and they knew not who it was that had taken them.

The moment he saw Angus and Duncan hanging by their necks, he *might* be inclined to keep his promise and let them go. Mayhap he'd kill them, just to be safe. But not before he had a little fun with Isobel. She was a beautiful woman. He wondered what she'd be like under the sheets. She was probably a tigress in bed.

He knew she wouldn't come to him willingly but it didn't really matter. He stifled a chuckle when he thought how Angus would take the news if he ever found out he had taken his precious Isobel against her will. But he couldn't stifle the chuckle that mental image brought.

Distractions. He could not afford them. He had to focus on the matter at hand. Kill Arline and get that stupid box from her. After that and after Angus and Duncan were dead, then and only then, could he take his pleasures with Isobel.

SEVENTEEN

A frown formed on Daniel's face when he saw that Lady Arline had slumped over on her mount, hugging the black mare's neck. A gently born woman such as Lady Arline was not accustomed to thundering across the country, through valley and glen, streams or forests. The journey was taking its toll on her.

He was not angry with her for falling asleep. He was instead angry at the circumstances that had put the girl in this situation. Daniel pulled his horse as close to Lady Arline's as he could and carefully took her mount's reins. He brought both horses to a slow stop so that he would not frighten her, causing her to tumble from her mount.

Moonlight shone down on her dark auburn locks casting streaks of silver through her hair. She was a beautiful young woman and he wondered silently what it was like for her to be married to such an auld man as Carlich. The auld man was not long for this world, even Daniel could see that. Mayhap, he thought, her next husband would be closer to her own age.

Though he had done his best to not surprise her too much, she woke with a start as soon as she felt them come to a stop. Her eyes flew open as she quickly scanned her surroundings, forgetting for a moment just where she was.

"I am so sorry, Daniel!" she exclaimed. "I did not mean to fall asleep. Why have we stopped?"

Daniel smiled, taking note that her words sounded slurred, tired. "M'lady, we stopped because ye fell asleep. It will do no one any good to have ye collapse from exhaustion. We can stop fer an hour or two so ye can rest."

Arline shook the cobwebs from her mind. "Nay, we'll not stop, Daniel. We must get to Stirling before dawn breaks."

Daniel let loose with an exasperated sigh. "But m'lady, ye'll do no one any good if ye fall asleep in front of the Stewart!"

"Is this not the day that your chief is set to hang?" she asked him sternly.

"Aye, but dawn is hours away, m'lady. And we be no' far from Stirling now. 'Tis why I suggested we stop and let ye rest."

While she could appreciate his concern over her wellbeing, she had made a promise not to be a bother to him or his men. Though it might very well have made sense to stop and rest, her conscience would not allow it. Every fiber of her being was telling her to get to Stirling as soon as possible. There would be time for rest later, *after* she had met with Robert Stewart.

"Nay, Daniel, we cannot stop now. I promise I shall rest after I do what my husband has asked that I do."

He had to admire her determination. "Have ye ever met Angus McKenna, m'lady? Or Duncan?"

Arline leaned over and took the reins from Daniel's hands. "Nay, I have not," she answered as she tapped the flanks of her horse. Daniel remained close by as they kept the horses moving at a slow pace.

"Angus be a good man, m'lady. He, all of us, will be forever in yer debt."

She felt rather uncomfortable at his proclamation. "I do not do this so that people will be indebted to me, Daniel."

A warm smile came to his face. "Aye, I ken that, m'lady. 'Tis one more reason why ye'll always be held in high esteem amongst our clan."

Arline was about to protest further when a shout of warning came from ahead. A moment later, flaming arrows began to land all around them, startling horses and riders alike. She had no time to react as her horse began to scream and rear itself up. A flaming arrow had hit the mare in the center of its chest!

With sword drawn in one hand, Daniel was able, with the other, to scoop Lady Arline from her mount before the horse could rear again. Her mare screamed in agony and the smell of burning flesh stung their senses. The beautiful animal reared again before taking off at a full run.

Daniel held onto Lady Arline rather precariously around her waist for a moment before setting her astride in front of him. Arline grasped the horse's mane tightly and held on for dear life.

The sound of metal crashing against metal, cursing, yelling and grunting broke through the night. Horses screamed as more flaming arrows lit the night sky before finding their marks in men and horses alike.

Bile rose in Arline's throat as the smell of burning flesh and blood found their way to her nostrils. Daniel had one arm wrapped tightly around her waist and held the reins betwixt his teeth as he fought off a mounted attacker to their right. Arline felt the rush of air as the tip of the attacker's broadsword whooshed by her leg. With his free arm, Daniel fended the man off with his broadsword. As the attacker lifted his weapon over his head, preparing to send it crashing down on Daniel's head, Daniel swept his sword across the man's arm and sliced his throat. Blood sprayed from the gash, landing across Arline's face, arm and leg.

Her heart pounded fiercely against her breast while visions of her own death whirled in her mind. She closed her eyes, but could not block out the sounds as the battle wore on. She felt Daniel's grip around her waist tighten as he spun the horse this way and that. He grunted and thrust, guiding the horse with the reins he still held in his teeth.

She realized that Daniel would not be able to fend the attackers off for long with the use of only one arm. Taking a deep breath, she opened her eyes and scanned the glen for either a place for her to hide or an opening for them to escape.

Bodies, dead or dying, littered the ground. Horses kicked and screamed, writhing in pain from the flaming arrows. Arline imagined no crueler fate could befall such beautiful animals and she cursed the attackers under her breath.

Daniel knew his first thought must be of Arline's safety. He *had* to get her to Stirling. But it was getting too difficult to battle the onslaught of attackers with just one free arm. Daniel had no doubt that the attackers were here for one thing and one thing only: Arline. Who they were or how they had found out about their mission to get her to Stirling he did not know. He prayed there would be an opportunity to sort that out later. For now, he had to protect her. If he could not defend himself, he could not defend Lady Arline.

His men had apparently come to the same conclusion as Daniel. Within moments, at least thirty of his men made their way through the attackers and came to surround him and Lady Arline.

Sweat poured into Daniel's eyes. He wiped his face against his shoulder as he tried to gain a better look at their surroundings.

David suddenly appeared beside them. He could see that blood covered both Daniel and Lady Arline. "Are ye hurt?" he shouted over the din of the battle. As the warriors stood surrounding Daniel and Lady Arline, they heard the sound of a familiar battle cry.

Daniel shook his head no as he studied the battle before him. "Nay," he shot back. "But they want the lady."

David gave a quick nod before bringing his horse as close to Daniel's as he could. "Get on," he commanded as he stretched out his arm.

Arline did not question his direction. She thrust her arm out and grabbed his just below his elbow. In one fell swoop, David swung her around and up to sit behind him. He did not need to tell her to hang on. Her arms went around his torso where she laced her fingers together and held on as tightly as she could.

David shouted a command before kicking his horse into a run. Arline closed her eyes again, praying with all her might that they would survive this night.

As they raced across the glen, Arline squeezed her legs tightly against the saddle and clung to David. Blood rushed in her ears and drowned out the din of battle and the horses as they ran across the land.

This was not the kind of adventure or excitement she had anticipated when she had agreed to go to Stirling. Nay, she had thought it might be fun to sleep out of doors under the stars and quiet moon. Being chased across the country by a group of men apparently wanting to kill her had not been even a remote thought.

With her eyes closed, she could not see what might be happening around her. But she could hear and feel. She felt the horse's hind legs burst with energy just before it jumped, or rather flew as if it had sprouted wings! Her stomach plummeted to her toes as she had the unexpected sensation of flying through the air. Time seemed momentarily suspended as she gasped and tightened her hold around David's waist. They landed without incident a short time later and the horse continued to speed across the land.

I'll never, ever, ever complain of boredom again! I'll never allow myself to daydream of adventure again! And I'll not let go of David until we reach Stirling.

EIGHTEEN

Wee William and his men had been on their way south of Stirling in search of either Angus and Duncan or clues to their whereabouts when they came across a battle. They had heard the ruckus before they were able to see it. Were it not for the full moon that shone brilliantly across the glen, they would not have been able to recognize the fact that it was MacDougall men being attacked.

Wee William gave a command to Black Richard to call the men to arms before he let loose with a battle cry. Moments later, he and his men swarmed down the small hillside and into the glen to help defend their brethren.

They took the offenders by surprise long enough for Daniel and David and the thirty men who surrounded them to break away from the battle. Wee William was momentarily caught off guard when he saw David flying by him at breakneck speed, with a woman behind him, holding on for all she was worth.

Within a quarter of an hour, Wee William and the rest of the MacDougalls were able to bring the battle to an end. Before all was said and done, most of the attackers were dead or slowly on their way to meet their maker. A few however, had fled. Whether it be in fear or in retreat to shore up more men, he could not know, for he had idea no why they had been attacked.

The moon was making its way across the sky. Wee William finally found Ronald and explained that Angus and Duncan were missing and that they had only stumbled upon the battle because they were trying to find the missing men.

Ronald was able to bring Wee William quickly up to speed on why they were here, where they were heading and what may have been the reason for the attack. When Ronald finished giving Wee William the details he was privy to, Wee William stood dumbfounded. Hopeful, yet dumbfounded at the turn of events.

"Yer certain, Ronald?" he asked as he ran a hand through his long red brown hair.

"Aye, I am. I heard it with me own ears. I am assumin' that David, Daniel, and Roy are takin' the lass to Stirling. I can only pray that no one else tries to stop them."

Wee William called after Black Richard. "See to our wounded, Black

Richard. Do what ye can fer them. As to these bastards, let the wolves have them!"

Black Richard gave a quick nod of his head before setting off to tend to the injured. Wee William found his horse and mounted. "Ronald, ye and yers come with us," he called out. "We must make certain the lady makes it to Stirling."

"But what of Angus and Duncan? It could be that the same bastards who attacked us took Angus and Duncan as well," Ronald said as he mounted his horse.

As Wee William saw it, he had only two choices. Wander the countryside in hopes of finding the two missing men only to come up empty handed. Or ensure that the lady made it to Stirling with the information that, if it didn't keep Angus and Duncan from hanging, would at the very least clear their good names. He looked around the battlefield and took a quick head count. Not too many of the MacDougall warriors had been wounded, at least not in comparison to the dead and injured offenders.

Wee William called out to Black Richard again. "Black Richard! When ye are done, continue to look for Angus and Duncan. And if ye find them, get them to Stirling as quickly as possible."

With the information that Ronald had given him, Wee William no longer dreaded getting his chief and friend to Stirling. At the moment, it might be the only safe place for any of them.

Taking no time to look back, Daniel, his men and Lady Arline tore across the glen. There was no way to avoid traveling through the forest that lay ahead. Going around it would put them further away from Stirling and closer to the assassins.

And assassins they were, of that, Daniel had no doubt.

Determinedly, Daniel led the group through the forest as fast as the terrain would allow. Occasionally, he would glance over his shoulder to see if anyone followed. He would not allow himself to breathe a sigh of relief until they were safely within the confines of Stirling Castle.

Lady Arline still clung to David, with her eyes closed tightly. For a gently born woman, she was handling herself quite well.

Anger formed deep in Daniel's gut as they ripped through the trees.

Greed. Whether it was the desire to amass power or money, it mattered not. A man could go mad for the want of those things. It was greed, plain and simple, that had put the proverbial nooses around Angus and Duncan's necks. It also put his own life, as well as the lives of his men and Lady Arline, in grave danger this night.

Come hell or high water, they would see that Lady Arline arrived safely in Stirling. Not only did the lives of Angus and Duncan depend upon her safe arrival, it was now quite evident that her own life depended upon it as well.

NINETEEN

It took Daniel a moment or two to realize it was Wee William's voice he heard booming through the night air. Daniel and his men spun around to meet Wee William and his men at the edge of the forest. The night sky was just beginning to wane. Dawn would be there soon enough.

"We'll talk while we ride, Wee William," Daniel told him. "We have to be at Stirling Castle before dawn breaks."

Both men looked east toward the horizon. Stirling Castle lay that way, just a few miles from where they stood. Their horses were covered in sweat, lathered and gnarled from the long ride and the battle fought earlier. Daniel worried that the horses would expire before they reached their destination.

Wee William nodded, sat taller in his saddle and raised his arm. He called out for his men to follow and a moment later, they were running like the devil was chasing them.

Daniel explained to Wee William the identity of the terrified lass clinging to David. Peeking through one eye, Lady Arline gave a curt nod of her head in Wee William's direction. Formalities be damned. She was not about to let go of David for fear they would fly through the air again. She was certain that her luck would not hold and the next time they jumped over something she would be tossed from the back of the horse.

A light mist clung to their skin and clothes. They were beyond damp from all the rain and streams they had ridden through. Arline knew she looked a mess and smelled even worse. She continued to make bargains with God. If He would allow her to live through this ordeal, she would never again complain of anything. She would be forever grateful for warm clothes, low burning fires, and even porridge.

As Arline made her bargains, Daniel and Wee William filled each other in on everything that had happened since they'd left Castle Gregor a fortnight ago. Wee William was just as surprised as Daniel and the others had been when they had learned what Carlich Lindsay had told them and what his wife now had in her possession.

After learning that the items Arline had hidden in her skirts might be just what was needed to keep Angus and Duncan from hanging, Wee William felt a sudden spurt of energy. Hope began to trickle back into his heart as they pounded across the land.

Wee William informed Daniel that the wagon bringing Angus and Duncan to Stirling had been set upon and that the two men had been captured. Now Daniel had something else to worry over.

They might make it to Stirling with the documents that would set the two men free but now, their futures looked even bleaker. Without knowing who had taken them and why, they were left with nothing but conjecture and guesses. Angus and Duncan could be anywhere by now. They could very well be dead.

And they still had no bloody idea where Isobel and Aishlinn were.

A spot on the horizon beckoned, urging them forward. Stirling Castle. They would be there soon, would deliver the documents to Robert Stewart, and then leave to join the search for Angus and Duncan.

They could only hope that mayhap someone in Stirling knew where Isobel and Aishlinn were. They could only pray that whoever had taken Angus and Duncan had not killed them yet.

They were far from being able to rest easy or have any sense of relief. The going back and forth between hope and despair made Daniel feel as though he were awash at sea, being carried to wherever the waves wished to take him.

Aye, the hanging delayed meant little to any of them for who knew what the dawn would bring with it.

TWENTY

Bree shook her head in complete disappointment. Her heart ached with guilt that she was actually taking her father and Duncan to Stirling. Reluctantly, she had surrendered to the arguments her father and Duncan had made. If they did not appear before Robert Stewart then it was quite possible that Isobel and Aishlinn would die, along with many others. No matter which way she looked at it, she would lose a parent.

If she refused to take her father to Stirling and Isobel and Aishlinn died, he would never forgive her and she'd never be able to forgive herself. The only way to keep Isobel and Aishlinn safe was to sacrifice the lives of her father and brother.

Och! How she wished Nial were with her. Aye, he would be more than angry that she had risked life and limb to rescue her father and Duncan. But she knew he would eventually forgive her for taking such a tremendous risk.

Her life, until Caelen McDunnah arrived at the McKee keep a week ago, had been blessed beyond comprehension. Nial loved her deeply, wholly, and passionately, without reserve. He was completely devoted to her. She had a beautiful son, a family she adored and loved, and a nice home. She wanted for nothing.

Now, her world was falling apart at her feet and she had never felt more alone. Emptiness had settled into her heart and she knew that her life had been forever altered. And for what? For one man's greed and need of power and another's sense of honor and duty.

That her father and brother were now willing to sacrifice their own lives in order that their wives would live was honorable. But now Bree knew the truth. It was not just for Isobel and Aishlinn that they were going willingly to the hangman's noose. It was for the good of their country.

She cast a glance at her father as they rode quietly toward Stirling in the wee hours just before dawn. Aye, she would take her father to Stirling, but she was in no hurry to make certain he arrived in time to hang.

Angus sat tall and proud in his saddle. Even with his filthy, tattered clothes, and the dirt that came from living in a dungeon these past weeks, he looked a formidable man. Bree choked on tears she refused to shed. She would not allow her father to see her cry. Come dawn, he would hang.

Robert and Collin rode ahead, next to Duncan. Bree kept to the rear, near her father. There were still so many questions she wanted to ask him but she doubted she had the strength to hear his answers.

Why he had done what he had done no longer mattered. When she had looked him straight in his eyes as he confessed all to her, she could detect no dishonesty on his part. Angus had bared his soul to her, had told her everything, the whole, sordid, ugly truth.

The only comfort she had was learning that Duncan had not been a part of this hideous scheme until the very end. Duncan had done what he had in the hopes that things would sort themselves out soon and in the end the truth would come to light. That hadn't happened and now it did not appear as though it would happen at all.

"Say what's on yer mind, lass," Angus said without looking at her.

Bree took a deep breath. She wanted to rant and rave, to scream, mayhap even to beat him over the head with a tree branch. She wanted to cry, to wail, to ask why. No child ever had a better father than she. No father ever looked upon his daughter with the adoration that Angus had with her. Even when she tried his patience, he had displayed nothing but patience.

Angus had taught her to defend herself, to think on her feet, and always help those who were less fortunate than she. In essence, he had been the perfect father to her, the perfect chief to their clan and the perfect husband to her mother.

Mayhap that was the problem. For her entire life she had held her father in such high esteem, had painted him as nothing less than perfect, even when *he* tried *her* patience. She had made him a god among men. Idolized him. And for the first time in her life, he had let her down. And not gently mind you. Angus McKenna was not as perfect as she had made him out to be. He was human.

"I love ye, da," she said sincerely. "No matter what happens on the morrow, I want ye never to ferget that."

Angus was quiet for a few moments, keeping his eyes on the land before him. "No man could ever have asked fer a better daughter than ye," he said. Bree noticed the slight break in his voice, as if he were choking back tears. "Never ferget that I was always proud of ye. Even when ye acted stubborn like yer mum."

Bree snorted softly at the mention of her mother. She knew her father was attempting to lighten the solemnity of the moment. "'Tis a good thing I have *her* temperament."

He finally turned to look at her. With a raised brow he asked, "Aye? Why is that?"

She looked ahead and smiled. "Fer if I had yer temper, ye'd have a verra bloody skull right now."

Angus chuckled and looked away. Bree had seen the moisture in his eyes when he had looked at her. It was that look, the look of pride and admiration that nearly did her in. No matter what he had or had not done, he was going to his death loving her. She would not allow him to go thinking she was ashamed of him.

The seriousness of the moment hit her with such force that it was all she could do to keep her seat. Never in her life had she felt such anguish or grief. She choked on her tears and did her best to maintain some of her dignity.

When she realized what they were truly discussing, she could not stop a few of her tears from escaping. The seriousness of it all, the solemn, grave truth of it was like a slap to her face. They were saying their goodbyes.

TWENTY-ONE

Unbeknownst to either the MacDougalls or those who had attacked them, there were other individuals near the glen that night. From the line of trees to the north of the melee, ten men silently watched as the violence erupted in the glen before them.

The silent watchers knew all about the MacDougalls and their mission. They also knew who it was that launched the flaming arrows and why.

Just as the MacDougalls' mission was to take Lady Arline to Stirling, the watchers were there to make certain that mission was accomplished. No one would think anything of the MacDougalls riding hell-bent-for-leather across the country trying to save their chief's neck. But ten strange men in black would have brought forth unwanted attention. Attention they could ill afford.

So the watchers, who lived in the shadows like apparitions, would not make their presence known. Anonymity was vital to their success as well as their lives.

The watchers had no wives, no children and no family but each other. They had sworn an allegiance, not to their king or their country, but to each other, much like King Arthur's legendary knights. Their fealty was to one another and an ideal, a pledge to defend against evil. They did not work for gold, fame, or fortune. Nay, it was far more sublime than that.

They trusted no one save for each other and the man who helped support their cause, the only other man on the earth who even knew of their existence.

They wore unremarkable clothing under their black cloaks. It made them look more like simple farmers than highly skilled warriors. Watching the attack unfold before them, they were just about to remove their black cloaks and come to the aid of the MacDougalls when they saw a large group of men approaching from the east. The leader of the watchers was about to call his men to arms when he realized it was more MacDougalls coming to the rescue. They also saw that Lady Arline was being whisked away to safety.

So they remained hidden and waited. The MacDougalls made quick work of their attackers and soon, the entire ordeal was over. The leader hoped that the MacDougalls wouldn't take time to bury the dead or question the living. He needed at least one of the living -- preferably one who did not like the idea of dying a slow, agonizing death and would gladly trade information for his life.

The leader sent five of his men to follow after Lady Arline, and two to search the area to see if they could perchance find a camp or more men sent to attack the MacDougalls. They had been searching for one man in particular for many days now. He supposed it was too much to hope that the bastard now lay among the injured. He could only pray that the MacDougalls would not recognize the man in question. He needed the man alive.

He had to make a decision and make it quickly. He could not risk the MacDougalls recognizing anyone. "We will need to go in," he whispered hurriedly to the man next to him.

Moments later, they were tucking their cloaks into their saddle bags and heading down toward the glen looking like nothing more than innocent farmers heading to Stirling for the festivities.

TWENTY-TWO

Wee William, Daniel, David and the rest of the MacDougall warriors made their way through the busy streets of Stirling. Although word had spread that Angus and Duncan had escaped -- or had been abducted -- it depended on which side of the fence you stood -- there were still hundreds upon hundreds of people milling about the streets. Mayhap people kept close to the gallows in hopes of seeing *someone* hanged this day. After all, many had travelled great distances just to say they were there they day they hung Angus McKenna.

The MacDougall men and Lady Arline rode up the narrow street that led to Castle Stirling. They passed by the gallows on their way, the sight of it making Wee William shudder. He prayed silently that God was watching over his chief and his friend.

Just as they passed the gallows, a commotion broke out in the crowd. A man cried out, "They found the McKenna! They found the McKenna!"

Wee William pulled his horse to an abrupt stop and tried to find the voice that shouted the news. Murmurs began to spread through the crowd. The people grew excited and louder, making it difficult for Wee William to hear what was being said. He dismounted and handed the reins up to Daniel. "Wait here," he told them as he set off to learn what he could.

The people had gathered around a middle-aged man who looked as though he enjoyed delivering the news and the attention it wrought. "I tell ye, I just came from the castle. Me wife works in the kitchens."

"So what?" someone challenged him. "Me son works in the stables. It doesna mean anything."

The news-bearer rolled his eyes and continued. "They found Angus McKenna and that traitorous son-in-law of his just moments ago. Aye, they'll still hang this day. Me wife says they'll hang before sunset."

Wee William felt his stomach fall to his toes. He resisted the urge to slam his fist into the face of the idiot who had called his chief and brother *traitors*.

"Is what they say true, Wee William?" Lady Arline asked from behind David.

"They seem to think it is," he said as he motioned toward the crowd. "We'll ken more when we get inside the castle." He prayed they would have an easier time gaining entry than when he was last here. If what the man had said was true and the hanging was taking place before sunset, then it was even more important that he see Robert Stewart. And if they were turned away, he would not hesitate to implement the plan he and Black Richard had plotted just yesterday.

Why they were being treated with more respect this day than the last time he was here, Wee William did not know, but he was grateful. Mayhap it was Lady Arline's status that helped them get past the guards at the gate of Stirling Castle. As it was, he didn't rightly care, as long as they could get an audience with Robert Stewart, the High Steward of Scotland. With King David held as prisoner by the English, Robert was the only man who could quash the death warrant issued by Phillip Lindsay.

If there were any truth to the rumors they'd heard in town, then Angus and Duncan were somewhere within these walls. Wee William would feel better if he could see the two of them with his own eyes.

What a sight Lady Arline and her warriors must have looked covered in sweat, blood, and mud. Wee William, Daniel, David, Roy and Ronald escorted Lady Arline into Castle Stirling. Lady Arline somehow managed to walk with an air of grace and refinement even though she was just as road weary and dirty as the large Highlanders who surrounded her.

What the five men could not see was that her insides were shaking. And had she not been holding firmly to Daniel's arm, she would have fallen more than once. She quietly debated on walking back to the Lindsay keep for she had no desire to ever ride a horse again.

They were taken to private quarters above stairs where three young maids offered a warm bath and clean clothes to Lady Arline. Arline began to protest that there was no time for such frivolities, though inside she was aching to wash away all the grime and filth and put on a fresh, clean dress.

"Mayhap, m'lady," the pretty little maid with the blonde hair offered with a shaky voice, "ye may want at least to wash up before meeting with his Lordship?"

Daniel and David cleared their throats as the other men tried their best to remain silent.

"Mayhap she be right, my lady," Daniel interjected. "'Tis been a verra long and trying journey here. Mayhap the Stewart would take us all a bit more serious if we didna look like heathens drug through the mud."

"Aye," David agreed. "I think we can take a few moments to at least scrape off some of the mud."

Arline supposed they were correct. "Fine, but we'll not tarry long!" she exclaimed. The sooner she met with Robert Stewart, the sooner she could return home.

Although she would have preferred to soak in the warm water until her skin wrinkled, there was no time for that luxury. The maids gave her strange looks when she refused to remove her leather necklace. It held the key to Carlich's box. She also declined their offer to have her gown cleaned. "Please leave it," she told the maids. "I shall tend to it myself."

From the looks the maids gave her she supposed they thought the gown should be burned instead of cleaned. The box Carlich had given her was hidden in a deep pocket.

The tub sat behind a beautifully decorated dressing screen and very near the fireplace. Carefully, she folded the dirty gown and laid it on a stool in front of the screen before sinking into the tub. It took monumental efforts her part not to fall asleep in the magnificently warm water.

Her thoughts were centered on what she would say to Robert Stewart when she finally met him. Would he listen? Would he believe her? Would he believe the authenticity of the documents? Silently she prayed that the documents inside the box were as important as Carlich had made them out to be and that they would prove Angus' innocence.

Maids came and went. Some brought more hot water while another brought tea and food.

Vigorously she scrubbed away the dirt and grime from her arms and legs. Her frustration and anger was beginning to get the better of her. Questions, most unanswerable at the moment, battered around in her mind. Why *had* Carlich sent her and not someone with more experience in political matters? Someone with more knowledge, tact, and more practiced in the fine art of diplomacy would have been a far better choice. Amongst her clan she was known for speaking her mind and not always in a thoughtful manner. She worried over saying the wrong thing or insulting Robert Stewart.

Once she was satisfied that she was as clean as she was going to be, she stepped from the tub and wrapped a long drying cloth around her shoulders. With little time to waste, she dried off hurriedly before stepping into a pretty green gown one of the maids had brought to her. 'Twas a bit short and a little tight in the bodice, but it was better than her own muddy and tattered dress. The satchel she had brought from home had been destroyed in the attack the night before. Arline's mind was on other matters and she had not bothered to ask from whom she had borrowed it.

She declined the offer to have the maid dress her hair and opted instead for a simple braid. She eased her feet into slippers that matched her gown, smoothed down the skirts of her dress and searched for pockets. She sent a prayer of thanks upward, for the dress had pockets and they were deep enough to hold Carlich's box.

The moment she lifted her dirty gown from the stool she knew something was wrong. It felt lighter. Dread pricked at her senses, sending goose pimples across her skin. Frantically, she thrust her hands into each of the pockets. Empty. She dropped to her hands and knees and searched the floor around the stool then widened the search to the rest of the room. Nothing under the bed, on the other side of the screen or under the chairs.

She knew the box had been in the dress before she stepped into the tub. She had triple checked it before folding it and placing it on the stool.

Good Lord, it was gone! Panic set in as she raced out of the room in search of the MacDougall men.

Wee William was just exiting one of the bedchambers as she ran down the hallway. It wasn't exertion that had her heart pounding and fighting for breath. It was fear.

"Wee William!" she cried out as she ran toward him.

The smile on his face faded instantly the moment he saw the look of fear on hers.

"It's gone!" she cried. "The box! It's gone!"

Wee William looked as though the wind had been knocked from his lungs. "Are ye sure?"

"Aye, I am sure! It was in my dress, not more than a few feet from me. When I finished my bath and went to put the box in the clean dress, it was gone."

"Well one of yer maids may have taken the dress!" Wee William sounded relieved.

"Nay!" Arline shook her head and wiped away tears. "The dress is there, but the box is not!"

Daniel, David and the rest of the men began coming out of the room when they heard the commotion. Arline quickly explained the situation. The dress was exactly where she had left it, but the box was gone.

"Who else, besides us, knew about the box?" Daniel asked to no one in particular.

"I did no' tell anyone," Arline told him as she dabbed at her eyes with the sleeve of her dress. "I told the maids to leave it. But there were so many people coming and going while I bathed. I was behind the dressing screen and could not see much."

"Do ye suppose one of the maids pilfered it, no' knowin' what it holds? Mayhap they think it holds jewelry?" David offered.

"I do no' ken," Arline said as she tried to settle her breathing. "I suppose 'tis plausible. But no matter who took it or why, we have to get it back."

The men split up into groups. Daniel and David went in search of all the maids that had entered the room while Ronald and Roy went to find guards who could help in the search. Arline went back to her room to search again. Wee William went in search of Robert Stewart.

He could only pray that Robert Stewart would delay the hanging long enough for them to find the damned box.

Each of the maids had been rounded up and now stood before Robert Stewart in his private chambers. Though the room was quite large and grand, it felt small. Seven maids stood before him while the rest of the room was filled with MacDougall warriors, a few of his guards, and the woman in charge of the maids.

Robert Stewart was of average size and build. Shoulder length, thick brown hair framed his long face with its wide-set eyes. He did not look happy, not at all happy. He sat in an ornately carved chair while he grilled each of the young women who stood before him.

Each of the maids denied any knowledge of the box let alone taking it. Even with his promise not to harshly punish whoever had stolen it, they continued to deny taking it.

After a quarter of an hour of grilling the maids, Robert Stewart reached the end of his patience.

"Fine. If ye canna be honest then each of ye shall be found guilty of thievery." He gave a nod to his guards. "Take them to the dungeon," he ordered. "They will stay there until we find the box."

The seven young ladies started to cry and plead innocence and beg for mercy. Robert Stewart would not be swayed.

The youngest of the maids, a girl of mayhap fourteen, burst into tears when one of the guards took her arm and began to lead her out of the room.

"Wait!" she cried. "I ken who has the box!"

The procession out of the room came to a rapid halt. The six innocent maids hissed their disapproval with the lass as the guard led the young girl back to Robert Stewart.

"The rest of ye may leave and go about yer business," Robert said to the remaining maids. They left in a hurried rustle of skirts and harsh whispers.

The young girl trembled as she stood in front of Robert Stewart. Tears streamed down her red cheeks.

"Where is the box, lass?" Robert Stewart asked, his voice calm. His cool demeanor belied the worry that he was actually feeling.

"I dunnae *where* it is, but..." she choked on a sob.

"But?" Robert asked.

"I ken who has it," she said, wiping the tears from her cheeks with her fingertips.

"Well?" Wee William chimed in. "Speak up lass!"

The girl jumped when she heard his voice. It all came spilling out in a rush of words, half of which they could not understand over her crying and sobbing.

"He said he would hurt me family if I didna get him the box!" she cried. "He said he kent where me family lived and if I didna get him the box, he'd kill them all and then me!"

Arline's heart sank. The girl hadn't taken the box thinking it was filled with jewelry. She hadn't stolen it for her own gain. She was terrified. Arline imagined she would have done the very same thing had someone threatened her family.

Arline went to her then and wrapped an arm around the poor girl's shoulder. "Wheesht, lass," Arline said. "We do no' think ill of ye. Just tell us who it was that threatened ye and told ye to get ye the box."

"I dunnae his name," the girl said.

A sigh of desperation and frustration filtered through the room. The MacDougall men were beyond irritated as evidenced by the scowls etched on each of their faces. Arline's hope wilted as her shoulders sagged. She had come all this way, had nearly been killed, only to have some stranger take it all away.

"I dunnae his name, m'lady," the girl whispered. "But I do ken what chamber he be in."

TWENTY-THREE

Within the hour, Arline and the MacDougall men were taken to a large gathering room below stairs. Dozens of people filled the elegant room. Men were dressed in their finest clothes and women looked as though they were attending a grand dance. The strangers huddled in small groups, whispering in hushed tones. Some cast curious glances at Arline and her warriors when they entered the room.

The MacDougall men surrounded Arline, watching her closely, hands on hilts of swords, eyes scanning the room. They were guarding Arline, on alert for even the slightest hint of trouble.

They had found the box and its contents in the room the young maid had taken them too. It had not taken long for Robert Stewart to learn who had been assigned that room. Aye, they had the box and knew who was behind the stealing of it, but they did not have the fool in custody yet. So the MacDougall men guarded her protectively. They would not let any harm come to the lady they had sworn to protect.

Throughout it all, Arline could not rid herself of the notion that Robert Stewart seemed familiar. She was quite certain that she had never met the man until this day, at least not formally. But there was something familiar in the way he walked and how he spoke. She could not quite put her finger to it and in the end, shrugged it off as nothing more than exhaustion.

She had been given a private moment with Robert Stewart and had explained all that she knew and all that Carlich had told her. He listened intently. Occasionally, he would give a nod of affirmation but not once did he ask any questions. Arline thought it more than a bit odd. Mayhap, she supposed, it was just the way Robert Stewart was and she warned herself not to read anything into his lack of questions.

They had been in the large gathering room for quite some time. Arline and her warriors declined the food and drink that was offered to them by the serving staff. Her stomach was in knots and she had no desire to throw up in front of anyone. The atmosphere of the room was not as somber as one would think. Nay, the people gathered were behaving as if they were at court and not the serious affair of deciding the fate of two men.

A sudden hush fell over the room when two large doors opened and a group of men entered. Some of them she recognized as guards who had helped in the search of the box. She had no idea who the others were. She watched in fascination as the group of men parted like the Red Sea to allow someone to walk through. It was Robert Stewart. He took the steps up to the dais without uttering a word and sat in the opulently carved chair. As soon as he sat, five men came to stand in front of him and faced the crowd.

"What the bloody hell?" Daniel muttered under his breath as he watched the five very familiar men come to stand in front of Robert Stewart. Rowan, Nial, Findley, and Caelen stood facing the crowd. Seamus Lindsay stood among them.

Arline's heart jumped to her throat when she saw Seamus. She tucked her hands into the pockets of her skirt and patted the box. Through no fault of her own, she had been thrust into this game of cat and mouse. Her role had changed suddenly, less than an hour ago. Now she must hide her fear, swallow it and not let it show. Innocent people were counting on her.

Wide-set eyes scanned the room before settling upon Lady Arline. She stood frozen in place for a moment before remembering her manners and offering her most elegant curtsy to Robert Stewart.

The people who had been milling about the room all came to stand closer to the dais.

Robert Stewart eyed the people for a few moments. His expression was unreadable. Uneasiness began to work its way into the pit of Arline's stomach.

"Bring them in," Robert Stewart finally spoke, directing his attention toward someone at the back of the room. The sound of his voice as it broke through the stillness of the room startled Arline, causing her to jump. David offered her his arm and a comforting smile. Gladly, she accepted both.

The hush that had fallen over the room was suddenly broken by the sound of excited whispers. Arline and the MacDougall men turned to see what had garnered their attention.

Ten heavily armed guards had entered. They walked on either side of Angus and Duncan who were shackled and chained together. Arline heard the MacDougall warriors gasp at the sight of their chief and their friend. Both men looked as though they had been dragged through mud and muck. Their clothes, hair and skin were filthy. Dark circles lined their eyes.

"Angus," Wee William whispered as the men walked by. They looked like hell. And how they managed to walk with their heads held high, Arline could not imagine.

They were taken to the front of the room to stand before Robert Stewart. Arline's heart pounded in her chest as she held her breath and waited.

"Angus McKenna and Duncan McEwan," Robert Stewart began, "more than a sennight ago, ye stood before the sheriff in Edinburgh, accused of crimes against yer king and country. Is that true?"

Angus and Duncan gave confirming nods. "Aye," they answered in unison.

A wave of whispers broke out among the people behind Lady Arline and the MacDougall men. Robert silenced them with a steely glare of reproach before he continued with questioning the two men.

"Ye were accused of consorting with known traitors. Is that also true?" Robert asked.

"Aye, we were accused of it," Duncan answered. The MacDougall men laughed at his answer. If his answer annoyed the steward he did a fine job of masking it.

"Angus, did ye or did ye not consort with known traitors?" Robert asked.

"Aye, I did." Angus' deep voice echoed throughout the room. The individuals in the crowd gasped in unison at his answer.

"And did ye also plot against king and country?"

"Aye, I did that too."

The whispers in the crowd grew louder. The tension was palpable. Arline looked at Daniel and David who stood on either side of her. Worry was etched into their faces as they stared ahead at their chief.

"Ye are sentenced to hang," Robert was stopped by the loud voices of Wee William, Daniel, David and the other MacDougall men who shouted in protest.

"Nay!" Wee William called out as he lunged forward.

"Be still, Wee William!" Angus shouted over his shoulder.

"I will no' be still, Angus!" Wee William said as he stepped to stand beside him. The guards quickly approached Wee William, their broadswords drawn. Within moments he was surrounded.

"Do ye wish to hang with the traitors this day?" Robert Stewart's voice was loud and firm, his question directed at Wee William.

Daniel, David, Ronald, and Roy all stepped forward. "Ye'll have to hang us with them!" Ronald shouted above the din of the crowd.

"Aye! Angus be no more a traitor than ye are!"

Arline stood alone now and panic began to settle in. More guards came rushing into the room and in short order all of the MacDougall men were surrounded. The crowd of onlookers had taken several steps back, but continued to watch. Arline worried that the men who had worked so diligently to keep her safe on the journey here would be dead before the sun set. As always, Seamus held the arrogant smile that she had grown to detest. He remained at the foot of the dais, watching silently and looking quite pleased.

While she did admire their fealty to their chief and their friend, Arline could no longer remain silent. She had to push her doubts over her role aside. If she remained quiet, said nothing, and did not give Robert Stewart the box, then these men *would* hang.

"Stop!" She managed to say but could not be heard over the rumble of the MacDougall men threatening to kill the guards and the loud murmurs coming from the onlookers.

"Stop!" Arline shouted again as she lifted her skirts and made her way to the steps of the dais. One of the five men standing in front of it stopped her from running up the stairs.

"Please let me speak," she pleaded with the tall dark-haired man who held her by her shoulders.

Robert stood and came to the edge of the dais. "That is enough!" he shouted over the roar of the room. All eyes turned toward him and the room eventually quieted. Robert turned his attention back to Arline. "Who are ye?" he asked with a barely noticeable smile.

With shaking legs she managed another curtsy. Aye, he knew her, but there were people in this room who were not aware of that fact. "I am Lady Arline Lindsay, wife of Carlich Lindsay."

Seamus stepped forward and came to stand by Arline. He took her hand and placed it in the crook of his arm, smiling down at her as if he were an adoring father figure. Arline knew him to be no such thing.

"My lord," Seamus began. "I do no' ken why she is here. Mayhap I should speak with her alone to learn why she has chosen to disrupt these proceedings."

He was not asking for Robert's permission. He was quietly demanding it. Arline began to tremble again when he placed his icy hand over hers and started to take her away. Instinct told her that she could not, under any circumstance, leave this room with him.

"Nay!" she shouted as she tried pulling away from him. He tightened his grip and refused to let her go. "I will no' leave!"

"Leave her be, Seamus!" Daniel shouted as he tried to step forward. One of the guards stopped him and would not allow him or any of the other MacDougall men to pass or come to Arline's aid.

"Speak, lass," Robert said as he stepped down from the dais. Gently, he took her hand and led her up the stairs. Seamus reluctantly let her go.

Arline could feel everyone watching her. Summoning her courage, she began to speak in a low, shaky voice. "Mayhap, my lord, we should speak in private." She was uncertain she could do what she must with Seamus standing so near and looking as though he could slice her throat.

Robert shook his head. "Nay, lass. Say what ye must and say it here."

Arline cast a sideways glance at Seamus, swallowed hard, and willed her legs to quit shaking. She lifted her chin and tucked her hand inside the pocket of her dress. "My lord, I bring ye something from my husband, Carlich Lindsay."

Robert tilted his head slightly. "And what is it ye bring from him?"

"Documents that ye may find important, as they pertain to Angus

McKenna's guilt or innocence."

Murmurs erupted through the room again. Arline wrapped her fingers around the box hidden in her pocket. If she kept her wits, this would all be over in a matter of moments and she could return to her home and her husband.

"This is absurd," Seamus decreed. "My father is a verra auld man, my lord. He hasn't left his room in months for he be far too ill. He's prone to exaggerations and fancies himself still a young man. I mean really, my lord," Seamus looked directly at Arline, as if he were ashamed of her. "Look at the young girl he has married!"

A few people in the crowd chuckled but Arline found no humor in it. Some may have found the marriage between she and Carlich odd simply due to the vast difference in their ages. Seamus had never hidden his displeasure over the marriage and she found his shame toward her exhausting.

"That is true, my lord," Arline said to Robert. "My husband *is* quite auld. And he is quite ill. But he is still of sound mind and heart, which is more than I can say for some of the people in this room."

Robert chuckled at Arline's comment, as did most of the people in the room.

"She is just as foolish as me father is!" Seamus seethed. His face had turned quite red and he was clenching his fists.

"And do ye have these documents with ye now?" Seamus asked with a brow raised arrogantly.

Arline lifted her chin and turned to look at Seamus. "The documents were kept in a small wooden box that my husband gave me. Two hours ago, someone stole that box from my room."

The crowd erupted into loud whispers. The MacDougall men looked murderous and quite anxious to get their hands on the man who was behind this sordid plot.

"Stolen, ye say?" Robert feigned surprise.

Seamus cocked his head to one side, clasped his hands behind his back and smiled at Arline. She wished she could be given the opportunity to wipe that smile from his face.

"My lord," Seamus said looking at Robert. "I must apologize fer me step-mother. I'm afraid she is just as daft as me father is. No such documents exist. She comes here bearing nothing more than stories told by a dying auld man."

"They are not stories, my lord," Arline said boldly before turning back to Robert Stewart. "The person who stole the box is a coward of the worst sort. He cares not if innocent people die for he is only motivated by greed." She turned back to Seamus and stared him directly in the eye. "I know who stole the box, my lord."

Seamus' countenance changed immediately. His eyes darkened with anger and his face paled before turning a deep crimson.

"I really must insist that we stop this nonsense at once," Seamus growled. "Angus and Duncan have already admitted their guilt. Why do we delay in hanging them?"

"What is yer hurry, Seamus?" Wee William asked.

"There is no sense in delaying justice!" Seamus barked. "They've had their trial, they've admitted guilt, and they've been sentenced. And they escaped! There are death warrants issued for all those who aided in that escape!" He paused for a moment and to regain his composure. "Ye MacDougalls are turning these proceedings into a farce."

"Calm yerself, Seamus Lindsay," Robert said calmly. With a wave of his hand, he called a guard forward. The man bent low so that Robert could whisper. The guard nodded and quit the room in a hurry.

Seamus turned back to Arline. "If these documents truly exist then they are forgeries and lies. I accuse ye, Arline Lindsay, of fabricating lies fer yer own gain." He turned back to Robert Lindsay. "Ye canna give any credence to what this liar says, my lord!"

His insults stirred Arline's anger. "I have proof, my lord," she said calmly. "I was able to find the box." She pulled the box from the pocket of her dress and handed it to Robert Stewart.

"She should hang with Angus and Duncan!" The calm demeanor Seamus was known for had rapidly faded. His face turned deep purple and spittle formed in the corner of his mouth. He took a step back and away from the dais.

Quickly, Arline lifted the necklace over her head and handed it to Robert. He opened the box and pulled out a scroll and gave it a quick glance.

"That document is the agreement between King Charles of England and the true traitor to the crown of Scotland. He agrees to give vital information to Charles, to insure that our men die in battle. He also promises to give names and locations of our fighting men. He gives that information in exchange for lordship over all the Highlands," Arline said as she raised her voice to be heard over the loud voices of the crowd. "And if the traitor brings King David's head to Charles, the traitor will be made King of Scotland."

The crowd erupted. Gasps of disbelief, shock and surprise flooded the air. Robert raised his hand in an effort to quiet them. "And whose signature is it on this document?"

Arline turned to face Seamus. "Aric Lindsay," she said. The crowd erupted once more before Robert again demanded their silence. The tension in the room was palpable. It hung in the air as thick as early morning mist. The MacDougalls wanted nothing more at the moment to get their hands on Seamus, for he had known the truth all along and did naught to stop his son.

More guards filed into the room, escorting a very angry Aric Lindsay. He, too, was set in chains. He had apparently put up a good fight for there was a large bruise along his jaw and his lip was swollen. Dried blood crusted on his chin. The guards brought him to stand before Robert.

Arline pulled another document from the box. Her anger energized her. Without unfolding it, she spoke again. Her voice was loud and calm and it surprised her that she had found the courage to stand in front of these people. "This document is nearly identical to the first. And on it is the signature of Seamus Lindsay."

"Those are forgeries! Lies!" Seamus shouted as he took another step away from the dais. "I refuse to listen to anymore of the whore's lies! She forged these for her own gain! The MacDougalls brought her here, without a female chaperone! Lord knows how many of them she spread her legs for!"

That insult was enough to get the MacDougalls angry enough to push through the wall of guards. Nial, Caelen, Rowan, and Findley had reached Seamus before the MacDougall men could. With swords drawn, they had the man pinned against the wall.

"Ye so much as blink and I'll run ye through ye bloody bastard." Nial ground out as he pressed his arm across Seamus Lindsay's chest.

"She lies!" Seamus cried out. "She's nothing more than me father's whore!"

Caelen had to hold Ronald and Daniel back to keep them from killing the foolish man.

"She may be a whore, but she speaks the truth!" Aric called out from across the room. Arline could only surmise that Aric smiled because he had lost his mind.

In three strides, Wee William reached Aric, grabbed him by his neck and tossed him across the room. He slid along the floor and landed next to his father.

"I told ye we should have killed the bastard when we had the chance!" Aric shouted at his father. "But ye wouldna let me!"

"Shut up Aric!" Seamus managed to yell.

"I told ye Angus was a spy! I told ye and told ye!" Aric spat at his father. "But ye would no' listen! Ye believed the lies he told!"

Seamus was trying to catch his breath. Sweat rolled off his forehead and into his eyes. Still, he could see Aric from the corner of his eye, smiling, laughing like a mad man.

"I told ye at Neville's Cross! I told ye it was Angus who stopped me from killing David! But ye would no' listen! Ye be a fool!"

It was all a blur after that. MacDougall men swearing, cursing Seamus and Aric, trying to kill the men with their bare hands. Two of the guards were accidentally knocked to their buttocks when they attempted to keep the MacDougall men at bay.

Angus and Duncan had remained shackled and did nothing to bring their men under control. They were positively relieved to know that they themselves would not hang today. It had been a very long few weeks they had endured. Quietly, they sat side by side on the steps that led up to the dais.

"Should we stop them, Angus?" Duncan asked with a yawn.

"Nay," Angus said as he stretched out his legs. "I do no' care how the two bastards die, just so long as they die." He let out a heavy, relieved sigh. Suddenly, he jumped to his feet, yanking a surprised Duncan with him. He ran toward the melee and shouted. "Stop!"

The MacDougall men, along with Rowan, Caelen, Nial and Findley came to an abrupt halt. Wee William had just pulled back his arm to send it into Seamus' Lindsay's face again.

"They have Isobel and Aishlinn!" Angus said. "If ye kill them, they canna tell us where they be!"

Wee William growled as he turned his attention back to Seamus. "Where are they?" He demanded.

Seamus, his face bloody, shook his head. "I'll die before I tell ye!"

"Go ahead and kill him!" a voice shouted from the back of the room. All heads turned to see who had made that challenge.

The crowd had turned away from the fighting and toward the back of the room. "Let me pass, ye eejit!"

Nial felt his stomach fall to his toes. He knew that voice, knew it all too well and he could not remember ever feeling so relieved to hear it!

A moment later, Bree pushed herself through the throng of onlookers. She took one look at her husband and ran to him. She flung herself into his open arms. With his broadsword in one hand, he pulled his wife in.

"Damn it, Bree!" he whispered hoarsely. "Ye gave me such a fright!"

Bree hugged him a moment longer before pulling away from his embrace. She looked up at her husband and smiled. "Ye can kill the bloody bastards."

"Bree!" Angus, Duncan and Nial chastised her foul language in unison.

She would not be deterred. "Och! Now is no' the time to be worryin' about me language. I say ye may kill these men and ye may kill them now."

"Bree, we dunnae where yer mum and Aishlinn be!" Angus told her.

Bree's smile widened. "They be fine!"

Another commotion broke among the crowd. Moments later, Aishlinn and Isobel made their way through the crowd of onlookers.

Angus nearly fell to the floor with relief. Duncan tried to race to his wife, but he was stopped short by the unmoving Angus who was frozen in place. Aishlinn ran to her husband not caring at all that he was filthy and smelled like he'd been sleeping with pigs.

Isobel ran to Angus with tears of joy streaming down her face. She wrapped her arms around his neck and held him close. The shock of seeing his wife, alive, and unharmed was too much. Angus collapsed on the floor, bringing his wife to his lap and pulling Duncan and Aishlinn along with them. Nial and Bree held on to one another, sharing kisses and hugs of relief.

"Ye are in a fair amount of trouble, wife, fer scarin' the life out of me," Nial told her.

Bree looked up at him innocently. "Whatever do ye mean, husband?" she asked.

"Ye ken *exactly* what I mean," he said before planting another kiss on her lips. "I saw ye and Maggy's boys attack the guards. I ken it was ye that stole yer father away."

Bree's face burned red for a moment. "I dunna what ye speak of, husband. Ye must be confusin' me with someone else."

"If I did no' think yer da would kill me, I'd turn ye over my knee right now and paddle that round little rump of yers," Nial said. He leaned in and whispered in her ear. "But I'll save that fer when we are alone."

Many tears were shed, kisses shared, and hugs given between the two couples huddled on the floor. They paid no attention to the crowd, the guards, or anything else. The only thing they cared about were their spouses.

Robert was able to talk Wee William out of killing Seamus and Aric on the spot, but he had to promise him he could put the nooses around their necks.

Seamus was put into shackles and he and his son were led to the dungeon. They would hang on the morrow.

Arline quietly left the room and made her way back to the bedchamber she had been given. She felt very much the outsider as she looked at Angus and Isobel and Duncan and Aishlinn and Nial and Bree. A flutter of something very unfamiliar went through her stomach in those moments before leaving them to their sweet and tender reunions.

She wanted to experience the kind of love and devotion she saw between the three couples. Her heart ached with wanting a man who would love her so much that he would be willing to sacrifice his own life in order to save hers. Aye, Carlich loved her, but not in any romantic sense. Nothing like the fiery passion she saw in Aishlinn's eyes, or Isobel's or Bree's. And their husbands openly, almost wantonly, returned those fiery, passionate looks.

Arline felt certain that nothing like that kind of love and adoration lay in her future. If Carlich died before she reached the age of one and twenty, she would be sent back to her father. Considering the condition Carlich had been in when she had left she would be surprised if he were still alive when she returned.

Slowly, she climbed the stairs and wound her way through the corridors of Stirling Castle. She made a wrong turn and had to back track twice, but finally and with much relief, she found the correct corridor.

As she walked down the hallway, lost in thoughts of regret and a huge sense of longing, she barely noticed someone walking toward her. It was the tall handsome man with dark hair, the one who had first stopped her from climbing the steps of the dais to Robert.

"My lady!" he said as he smiled and approached. Arline paused just outside her door. She wanted nothing more than to escape into the bedchamber and get some much needed sleep.

"My lady," he said with a smile, flashing a dazzling set of perfect teeth. "I just wanted to thank ye, fer what ye did fer Angus and Duncan."

Arline smiled up at the braw man. "Think nothing of it, sir." He was a most handsome man. Nay, he was beyond handsome. Thick dark hair hung to his broad shoulders. Deep brown eyes glistened in the torchlight. Arline could not remember ever seeing a more handsome man. She took a deep breath and tried to concentrate on what he was saying.

"Nay, my lady," he said. "'Twas a verra honorable thing ye did. Daniel and David tell me that ye are a woman possessed of the utmost honor and heart. Because of ye, Angus and Duncan have been proven innocent and will get to spend the rest of their days with their wives."

Arline could only nod her head. If ever a man could be considered beautiful, it was this man. Were her husband Carlich as young and as handsome as the man standing before her, she would probably never want to leave her bedchamber. She felt her face burn with embarrassment and quickly turned away from him. "That is most kind of them to say. If ye will please excuse me, I am verra tired."

"Aye, my lady, but please," he said as he reached out and touched her arm. "Please ken how much not only the MacDougalls but me own clan, Clan Graham, appreciate all that ye've done."

Arline nodded again and took a chance to look at him one more time. "'Twas the right thing to do, sir."

He threw his head back and laughed. An odd sensation swept over Arline. His laugh, for whatever reason, warmed her heart. "Aye, me wife says that verra same thing when I give her thanks fer goin' above and beyond what others would!"

Why she suddenly felt sorrow at learning he was married, she could not begin to comprehend. She, too, was married, but somehow that felt different. Carlich was, after all, a very auld man. Nonetheless, guilt tugged at her conscience.

She offered him a polite smile and bid him goodnight before slipping into her room. Sleep would not come easy, not with the image of a handsome man with dark hair and deep brown eyes floating around in her mind.

TWENTY-FOUR

"'Twas ye, wasn't it?" Arline asked pointedly. She had slept the day away and had not awakened until long after the evening meal. The castle was quiet for most everyone was tucked away for the night.

She stood now, alone in Robert Stewart's private chamber for the third time that day. He sat quietly in a chair near the fireplace. Arline stood but a few steps away from him, her hands folded in front of her.

It had come quietly to her, in her dreams, just who the mysterious man in the shadows of her husband's bedchamber was. She stood now, in front of the accused, waiting patiently for his admission.

Robert eyed her closely for a minute, but said nothing.

"'Twas ye in Carlich's chamber that night, my lord. I am certain of it."

"Now, why would I be in yer husband's bedchamber, my lady?"

Arline tilted her head slightly before answering. She tried to appear nonchalant, as if the revelation wasn't as important as it actually was. "I ken that ye and my husband are verra good friends. I also ken that my husband respects you, my lord. He holds ye in the highest regard."

Robert had no response. He took on that same indifferent air that Arline held. He rested his head against his index finger, and appeared unmoved by her statement.

"Ye have a certain gait to your walk, my lord. Even though ye had remained in the shadows and did not allow me to see your face, I ken, without a doubt, that ye *were* in my husband's chamber just days ago."

"Tell me, my lady, what else is it ye think that ye ken?"

Arline took a deep breath as she took a step closer to the fire. "It was ye that gave Carlich the documents."

Robert blinked once, then again. "Now, why, pray tell, would I do such a thing?"

"We ken that there is no love loss between ye and Seamus, my lord. If ye had presented the documents, people might have believed his accusations that the documents were indeed forgeries. However," she paused briefly, choosing her words carefully. "If the documents came from his own father, or me acting on behalf of his father, then people would give it more credibility."

Robert shifted in his seat, crossed his legs, and bade her to continue with a wave of his hand.

"So it could no' be known that ye had the documents. Angus was working for you. I imagine, though I could be wrong, that it was Angus who gave ye those documents. I ken that Aric mentioned Neville's Cross. What happened there, my lord?"

Robert took a deep breath before he answered. "Neville's Cross," he said the name woefully. "Things were going verra well fer us, until Neville's Cross. 'Twas there that Aric tried to kill King David."

Arline gasped, her eyes widened with shock. "Oh, Good Lord!" she exclaimed breathlessly.

"Aye. Had Angus not been there, had he not been just a few steps from David, then Aric would have been successful. Angus saw Aric come fer David. Angus had tried his best to push David out of the way, but Aric's blade managed to cut him. Angus was able to convince Seamus that it was no' yet the right time to take David's life and that is why he stopped Aric from killin' him. While Angus was busy with Seamus and Aric, Duncan managed to get David to cover, under the bridge at River Browney while he went to get help. There was so much chaos happenin' at the time, that we're no' quite sure what happened after that. But we think 'twas Seamus who found King David and led the English to him."

Arline felt her legs growing weak and she sat down in the chair opposite Robert's. "I never trusted Seamus. Och! The clan adored the man. But there was something, something I could not quite put my finger to. It made me no' trust him. Or Aric."

"Yer instincts are good, lass. Ye might want to always listen to them."

Arline sat quietly for a time, stunned at what Robert was telling her. When she thought how close she had come to dying just a few days ago, when she and the MacDougalls were attacked, she shivered.

They stared at one another for several long moments before Arline spoke again. "Who is the man in the shadows now, my lord? The one standing in the corner near your curtains?"

Robert raised an eyebrow. "Yer powers of observation are verra good, my lady. The identity of the man who stands in the shadows is of no importance to ye. But ken that there may be more traitors among us. Men who worry that Seamus or Aric will talk. These men might not take too kindly to ye givin' me those documents." Robert stood and came to stand before her. "Ken this well my lady. Until we ken for certain that we have *all* the men involved in this event, ye might no' always be safe. There will always be a man in the shadows, watchin' over ye, to ensure that ye are kept safe."

She felt the sting of fear deep in her belly. *It is not over.*

"A few weeks ago," Robert's voice broke through her quiet thoughts. "Aric convinced his uncle, Phillip Lindsay, that Angus was the true traitor in all of this. That is when Phillip had Angus and Duncan arrested and taken to Edinburgh. While they were arresting them, Aric and his men kidnapped Isobel and Aishlinn. What Aric and Seamus didna ken was that Phillip kent the truth. Phillip had been workin' with us."

She couldn't fathom why that bit of news surprised her. It was difficult to think that someone she had lived with for the past three years was capable of such nefarious deeds. Nay, she never liked Aric or his father. But she had always assumed it was because neither of the men hid their distaste of her.

"How did they come to be here today?" Arline asked.

Robert smiled at her. "The men in the shadows, lass. They'd been watching Aric and Seamus. They were there the night they took Isobel, Aishlinn and the babes. They were able to steal them away from the hut they were held prisoner in, just as soon as Aric and Seamus left. I've had the women and the babes here, at Stirling, for weeks now. But I could no' let anyone, no' even Angus and Duncan ken that. No' until I could prove, without a doubt, that Aric and Seamus were guilty."

"That is where I came in." Arline stated solemnly.

"Aye, lass. That is where ye came in."

"It was Aric or Seamus that attacked us, wasn't it?" she asked quietly.

"Aye, 'twas Aric. But the men in the shadows were there that night as well, watchin' over ye. But as it turned out, the MacDougalls kept their word and did no' let any harm come to ye. They be good men, lass. Ye can always count on them as ye can count on me, should the need ever arise." He placed a hand on Arline's shoulder.

"Ken this, my lady. I will always be here to help ye in yer time of need. I will always keep a man in the shadows near ye. Ye won't ken who he be. But he will be there." Robert walked to the desk that sat in front of the tall windows. He opened a drawer and pulled out Carlich's box along with the key. He brought the items back to Arline.

"Ye return Carlich's box to him now, my lady. Inside it, I have placed a letter, with me seal affixed to it. Should ye ever find yerself in trouble and ye canna find or see the man in the shadows, use this letter."

Reluctantly, Arline took the box and the key from him. She slipped the box into the pocket of her skirt and held the key in her hand. She knew it was a false sense of security she had in the letter, still, she was glad for it. The letter itself could not actually keep someone from slicing her throat, but, who knew if or when it would ever become useful.

"Now," Robert said as he turned away. "On the morrow ye will be returned to Carlich. Ye will have a full escort of me men to see ye safely returned."

He was done discussing the matter. Arline began to wonder if she would ever again feel the bliss of safety.

Robert turned back to her. "Scotland thanks ye, my lady. As does King David."

Arline left the room as quietly as she had entered. She wondered if the man in the shadows was going to follow her back to her room. She was uncertain if that thought brought comfort or fear. If the men in the shadows were near her then danger could not be far behind.

She could only pray that someday she would be able to live her life without looking over her shoulder, without wondering if someone was lurking in the shadows, watching, waiting for the right moment to strike.

Arline had a decision to make. She could live her life in fear of the unknown, or she could live as if she had not a care in the world. Good sense told her to live her life as best she could, but keep an ever vigilant and watchful eye. A watchful eye that would look to the shadows for help if needed and answers when necessary.

EPILOGUE

Carlich Lindsay had kept his word. He waited until a week after Arline returned before finally succumbing to old age and disease.

Before he died he asked Arline to write a letter to Phillip. "I have many regrets," he told her. "I want Phillip to ken that my biggest regret is not seeing all the good in him and ignorin' him when he was a child. I should have listened to his mum. I should have enjoyed his creative mind instead of worryin' over what others thought. I ken it be too late now, to make up fer it, but I need him to ken it."

Arline knew that the depths of Carlich's guilt could not be felt or seen in a letter. She had hoped that Carlich would live long enough to tell Phillip himself. Phillip had sent a letter to his father explaining that he could not leave his wife this close to delivering their first bairn. Unfortunately Phillip would not arrive in time to hear his father's words of regret.

Seamus and Aric's deaths also weighed heavily on Carlich's heart. It wasn't just a father's guilt for knowing he helped hang his oldest son and grandson. "I spoiled him too much," Carlich had told her. "'Tis me own fault fer allowin' him too much freedom. Had I been firmer with him, mayhap he would no' have chosen the path of treachery."

Arline would not allow her husband to feel any guilt over the choices his son and grandson had made. "Do no' go blamin' yerself, husband!" Arline chastised him. "Seamus made his choices. He let greed cloud the good judgment that I be sure ye taught him."

Arline knew he had tried to hang on, wanting desperately to see Phillip one more time. Guilt and regret, along with auld age claimed its final toll when Carlich passed away just after dawn on a sunny summer morning. Her heart ached with sadness at his passing.

While Phillip regretted not being able to make amends with his father, he did not regret being there for his wife when she gave birth to their beautiful little girl. The babe came screaming into the world on the eve before Carlich passed away.

Phillip and Helena waited two months before embarking on the long journey to the Lindsay keep. He was laird now, chief to his clan. He hadn't any good idea how to make the transition from a solitary man to one whom hundreds of people now relied upon as their leader. He wasn't good at that sort of thing, hadn't had any training on how to be a good laird. But with Helena at his side, he felt confident that he could rise above his own self-doubts and be a good chief to his people.

The death of Liza, the sweet young kitchen maid, had left the clan in a deep state of mourning. They had to assume that it had been Seamus or Aric who had killed her for they could not believe anyone else would have done such a thing. The clan took some measure of satisfaction in knowing that when the two men were hanged for their crimes against king and country, they paid for the death of Liza as well. The clan grieved over her loss as much as they grieved over Carlich's. But not one tear was shed for the men responsible for thrusting their clan into such despair and turmoil.

Arline's father had sent a small group of men to escort her back to Ireland. They arrived the same day as Phillip and Helena. Arline had pleaded with her father's men to allow her a few more days, for time to spend with the couple and their precious babe. Her pleas for time were denied. They would leave on the morrow at first light.

"Yer father insists that we return with you immediately, m'lady," her father's first lieutenant explained.

Arline knew all too well that her immediate return did not signify that her father missed her. There was a very strong possibility that he was already in the process of finding her another husband. At least she would have a year of mourning before being forced into another marriage. Hopefully, her next husband would be younger, but she would settle for someone kind like Carlich.

With what little time they had together, Arline did her best to explain to Phillip the regrets and guilt Carlich had struggled with.

"Forgiveness is no' an easy thing to ask for, and at times 'tis even more difficult to give," Arline told Phillip as she handed him Carlich's last letter.

They stood on the steps of the keep in the brilliant sunshine. Helena stood beside her husband, holding their daughter. Love for her husband was plainly evident in Helena's eyes. *Mayhap*, Arline thought, *Helena can help him to see the truth.*

"If he had to do it all over again," Arline explained, "He would have done things verra differently."

The doubtful expression on Phillip's face said he did not believe her. Mayhap it *was* too little, too late. With a heavy, anguished heart, Lady Arline left Phillip, Helena and the babe on the steps.

She had already said her goodbyes to Fergus, Meg, and the rest of her people. Fergus had tried to offer her hope that all was not lost. "Ye'll return someday, I ken it," he told her with a broad smile. As much as she wanted to believe him, her heart told her otherwise. Instead of arguing, she gave him a firm hug and whispered thank you into his chest.

Her father's lieutenant held the reins to a black gelding. With help from the stable master, she was soon mounted and leaving the one place she had ever felt at home or at peace.

There was comfort knowing that she had Robert Stewart's letter and the men in the shadows. Combined, those two forces could prove quite useful in the future. Deep down however, she prayed the need to use them would never arise.

She took with her many happy memories of Carlich, Fergus, and her people. Her father might be able to take her from Scotland but he would never be successful in taking Scotland from her heart. Tucked securely away, like Carlich's box, she would keep her feelings for and memories of this place well hidden. Only in times of sorrow or loneliness would she allow her heart to revisit them.

Along with those, was the image of the very handsome man, whose name she did not know. The exceedingly handsome man with the perfect teeth and brilliant smile was forever etched in her mind.

For whatever reason -- she could make no real sense of it -- she had decided to use that image to measure against any future husband she may acquire. She had convinced her heart that only a kind, gentle man of good character, temperament and patience could posses such a handsome face. That too, she would keep unto herself.

Losing Carlich left a gaping hole in her heart. More friend and grandfather than husband, still, she missed him. He had treated her with respect and dignity. Next to her sisters, he had been her dearest friend and closest ally.

Arline paid no attention to her father's men, six in all. They led her out of the gates of the keep and headed east. The beautiful morning, with the cloud free, brilliant blue sky stood in stark contrast to the ache in her heart.

They had not ridden long when they heard the sound of many horses charging from behind. They pulled rein and spun around only to see at least fifty men on horseback riding hard toward them.

"Ready your arms, men," the lieutenant ordered. Much to Arline's surprise, the men made no attempt to protect her. Instead, they formed a line *behind* her.

Arline's heart lodged in her throat with the memory of the night she and the MacDougall men were attacked. She glanced over her shoulder only to see that her father's men looked positively terrified. She cursed them all under her breath as she removed her sgian dubh from her pocket. She was fully prepared to defend herself, even if the cowards behind her would not.

Just as she was ready to shout that she would ride back to the keep for help, she caught a glimpse of a very familiar figure. He sat taller in his saddle than any of the men he rode with.

"Wee William," she whispered. She let out a relieved sigh and giggled. Shaking her head at the cowardice of her father's men, she urged her horse forward to meet the MacDougall men.

"My lady!" Daniel called out as the large contingent of warriors rapidly advanced.

Arline's heart lifted at the sight. She recognized the faces of Daniel, David and many of the other men who had seen her safely to Stirling. She was very glad to see them and wished that she could hug each and every one of them.

"Daniel," she called out in return. Moments later, she was surrounded. "What are ye doin' here?" she asked.

"We came to see ye, to offer our thanks once again," David explained. His smile evaporated when he looked at the six men who were supposed to be protecting their lady.

"Phillip says yer da sent men to take ye back to Ireland," Daniel said. He began to look just as angry as his brother when he saw Lady Arline's supposed protectors.

Arline laughed when she saw the ire building in the brave warriors expressions. She needn't ask them why they scowled and glared at her father's men. She was no more impressed with them than the MacDougalls.

"I fear I may end up havin' to protect *them* on my journey back to Ireland," she said with a wry smile.

Two men began to push their way through the pack. Arline barely recognized them, for they weren't shackled or covered in filth.

"I think the lass deserves a much better escort," Angus said with a frown toward the six men.

"Aye," Duncan agreed. He shook his head in disgust at the cowards.

Arline eyed the MacDougall men for a moment. Admittedly, her protectors left a lot to be desired. She knew without question that the MacDougall men would have formed a wall around her the moment they heard or saw strangers approaching. Apparently her protectors were not so inclined as to risk their lives for hers.

"Aye, they are no' much to brag over," Arline agreed.

Angus looked to Duncan first, then to Daniel and David before turning his attention back to Arline. "My lady," Angus said. "If it pleases ye, I think I could spare a few of me men to help escort ye back to Ireland. I canna go meself, but I believe I could find a volunteer or two."

For an extremely brief moment, she thought to decline his generous offer, but immediately pushed the thought aside. The last time she had ridden across the countryside, she had nearly been killed. If there were, as

Robert Stewart had alluded, more traitors in their midst, they might seek to kill her out of retribution for the deaths of Seamus and Aric. If she were attacked on her way back to Ireland, she had no doubt she would not survive when she considered her current six escorts. Besides, she doubted that the MacDougall men would have listened to her.

"That would be verra generous of ye," she said, accepting his offer. She scanned the group of men, looking for one man in particular. The handsome man with the brilliant smile. After a short time, she realized he was not with them. A slight pang of regret stung at her heart. 'Twas probably best that he wasn't here for she might learn that he wasn't as perfect as she had allowed her heart to believe.

When her six escorts finally realized the group of Highlanders presented no danger, they came to join them. Arline informed the lieutenant that several of the MacDougall men would be accompanying them on their journey back to Ireland. Seeing the fierce scowls and sheer determination on the faces of the MacDougall men, the lieutenant did not offer any argument against it.

Shortly thereafter, Daniel, David, Ronald and Roy surrounded Arline. A handful of other MacDougall men fell in behind them and rode with her father's men. For the first time in many weeks she actually felt happy and quite safe.

It would take at least two weeks for them to travel the long distance to her childhood home. Two more weeks of building wonderful memories that she would keep with her always.

Prologue Rowan's Lady

Scotland 1350

The Black Death did not discriminate.

Like fire from hell, it spread across England, Wales, Italy and France. Untethered, unstoppable.

It cared not if the lives it took were of the noble and wealthy or the lowly born and poor. It showed no preference for age or gender. It took the wicked and the innocent. It took the blasphemers and the righteous.

The Black Death took whomever it damned well pleased.

It took Rowan Graham's wife.

Rowan would not allow his sweet wife to die alone, cold, afraid, and in agony, no matter how much she begged otherwise. He would not allow anyone else to administer the herbs, to apply the poultices, or to even wipe her brow. He was her husband and she, his entire life.

Knowing that the Black Death had finally reached Scotland, Rowan's clan had prepared as best they could. The moment anyone began to show signs of illness, they were immediately taken to the barracks. Seclusion was their only hope at keeping the illness from spreading.

Within a week, the barracks could hold no more of the sick and dying. The quarantine was all for naught.

By the time Kate showed the first signs of the illness, the Black Death had taken more than thirty of their people. Before it over, Clan Graham's numbers dwindled to less than seventy members.

At Kate's insistence, their three-month-old daughter was kept in seclusion. It was the last act of motherly love that she could show her child. In the hours just before her death, Kate begged for Rowan's promise on two matters.

"Ye shall never be afraid to speak of me to our daughter. It is important that she know how much I loved her, and how much *we* loved her together." 'Twas an easy promise for Rowan to make, for how could he ever forget Kate?

'Twas the second promise she asked that threatened to tear him apart.

"And ye must promise ye'll let another woman into yer heart. Do not save it long fer me, husband. Yer too good a man to keep yerself to a dead woman."

He swore to her that yes, someday he would allow his heart to love another. Silently however, he knew that day would be in the very distant future, mayhap thirty or forty years. For there could never be a woman who could take Kate's place in his life or his heart.

"I love ye, Kate, more than me next breath," Rowan whispered into her ear just before her chest rose and fell for the last time.

Fires were built to burn the dead. When Rowan's first lieutenant came to remove Kate's body to add it to the funeral pyres, he refused to allow Frederick anywhere near her. Rowan's face turned purple with rage, his chest heaved from the weight of his unconstrained anguish. He unsheathed his sword and pinned Frederick to the wall.

"If ye so much as think of laying a finger to Kate, I shall take yer life," Rowan seethed. Frederick knew it was a promise Rowan meant to keep.

Later, with his vision blurred from tears he could not suppress, Rowan bathed his wife's once beautiful body now ravaged with large black boils. He washed her long, strawberry blonde locks and combed them until they shined once again. When he was done, he placed a bit of Graham plaid into the palm of her hand before wrapping her cold body in long linen strips.

Alone in the quiet hours before dawn he carried her to final resting place under the tall Wych Elm tree. He stayed next to her grave for three full days.

Frederick finally came to see him late in the afternoon of the third day.

"I ken yer grievin', fer Kate was a fine woman." Frederick said. "Ye've a wee bairn that needs ye, Rowan. She needs ye now, more than Kate does."

Rowan was resting against the elm tree, with his head resting on his knees. In his heart he knew Frederick was right, but that did nothing the help fill the dark void that Kate's death left in his heart.

For a brief moment, Rowan could have sworn he heard his wife's voice agreeing with Frederick. Deciding it best not to argue the point with either of them, Rowan took a deep breath and pulled himself to his feet.

For now, he would focus on the first promise he had made to Kate.

"Ye be right, Frederick," Rowan said as he slapped one hand on his friend's back while wiping away tears with the other. "I need to go tell me daughter all about her beautiful mum."

Rowan's Lady is set for release in October 2013.

ABOUT THE AUTHOR

Suzan lives in the Midwest with her verra handsome carpenter husband and the last of their four children: a 15 year old, 6'3", built-like-a-line-backer son. They currently accept monetary donations to offset the cost of feeding him and keeping him in shoes. She also has three perfect grandchildren.

Suzan has no pets, save for the aforementioned son and husband. Living where they do, she figures the domesticated deer who believe her gardens are planted strictly for their enjoyment is plenty. Though, if she lived on ten or more wooded acres she would have a Redbone Coonhound that she would name Rufus. She'd also like to be a size 12 again, but doesn't foresee either of those things happening at anytime in the near future.

"Some say my writing is an obsession. I prefer to think of it as a passion."

You may keep up to date with Suzan at:

Amazon Author Page
Facebook Fan Page
Suzan's Blog
twitter@suzantisdale

Made in the USA
Lexington, KY
17 April 2014